Phone Calls

from the Dead

PHONE CALLS

FROM THE DEAD

stories by Wendy Brenner

ALGONQUIN BOOKS OF CHAPEL HILL   2001

Published by
Algonquin Books of Chapel Hill
Post Office Box 2225
Chapel Hill, North Carolina 27515-2225

a division of
Workman Publishing
708 Broadway
New York, New York 10003

For permission to use quotations from copyrighted works, grateful acknowl-
edgment is made to the copyright holders, publishers, or representatives named
on page 228, which constitutes an extension of the copyright page.

This is a work of fiction. While, as in all fiction, the literary perceptions and
insights are based on experience, all names, characters, places, and incidents
are either products of the author's imagination or are used fictitiously. No
reference to any real person is intended or should be inferred.

Stories in this collection originally appeared in the following publications:
"Are We Almost There" in *Mississippi Review;* "Awareness" and "Mr.
Puniverse" in *Oxford American;* "The Cantankerous Judge" in *Carolina
Quarterly;* "Four Squirrels" in *CutBank;* "The Human Side of Instrumental
Transcommunication" in *Story;* "Nipple" in *Five Points.*

"Mr. Puniverse," "Nipple," and "The Human Side of Instrumental
Transcommunication" also appeared in *New Stories from the South.*

Library of Congress Cataloging-in-Publication Data
Brenner, Wendy.
     Phone calls from the dead : stories / by Wendy Brenner.
        p. cm.
     Contents: The human side of instrumental transcommunication—Nipple
—The anomalist—Four squirrels—Are we almost there—The cantankerous
judge—Mr. Puniverse—Mr. Meek—Awareness—Remnants of Earl.
     ISBN 1-56512-245-3
     1. United States—Social life and customs—20th century—Fiction.
     I. Title.
PS3552.R3863 P48 2001
813'.54—dc21   2001035537

10 9 8 7 6 5 4 3 2 1
First Edition

For their faith and support, I am grateful to the
National Endowment for the Arts.
Thanks also to Kathy Pories, Rebecca Lee, Jamie Arthur,
and, much belatedly, Angela Graham.

CONTENTS

Even then she wore the look of certain fanatics who think of themselves as leaders without once having gained the respect of a single human being.

—Jane Bowles, *Two Serious Ladies*

THE ANOMALIST

His Mission

His mission was simple: to destabilize scientific paradigms by assembling a multivolume collection of every scientific anomaly ever recorded—an *Encyclopedia of Anomalies,* the most comprehensive, exhaustively researched reference text of its kind. Okay, so maybe it wasn't simple—but it could be accomplished. It was not an experiment, in which the outcome was uncertain, but a task.

He loved tasks. He loved the gut satisfaction of collecting, going from empty to full, knowing you hadn't missed anything. Unlike his colleagues at the corporate labs where

2 ▸ WENDY BRENNER

he interned as a student, he never complained about working on the cash-cow research projects commissioned to prove
what was already known, the endless recording of data
in closed white rooms, no credit, no contact, no ground-
breaking results. Teachers and girlfriends had always told
him he was obsessive, "though not interestingly so," his college girlfriend, a poet, said. "Your imagination is so literal,
it's not even an imagination," she told him. "It's like, a
dresser or something."

"But you knew I was a marine biology major when we
started going out," he said. "Scientists have to be logical."

"Scientists are supposed to love competition, discovery,
not just data, data, data," she said, and then dumped him
for his art-major roommate, a natural extrovert who had
a high-paying museum curator job waiting for him upon
graduation, because, he bragged, "I interview like a mother-
fucker."

She had gotten on the anomalist's nerves, anyway, always announcing everything that was happening as it was
happening, the way old people did at the movies—so that
he secretly began to think of her as PA Girl. Like when they
were lying entwined, she would say, "We're so close right
now." After they ate she exclaimed, "We're done!" "We are

having so much fun," she'd say, and he'd think, *Yeah, I was, until the PA came on* . . . She wasn't so unusual, he knew; people seemed to love narrating their own lives, an urge he had never understood. So much in the universe still cried out for examination, explanation, or at least some *mention*, he didn't see why anyone would waste time pointing out the obvious.

He had begun, as a kind of hobby, clipping or copying items he found in the newspaper or in the old issues of *Scientific American* and *Nature* and *Sky and Telescope* he used for his term papers, accounts of anomalies that had been observed and recorded but never explained by science. *Electric Trees in Chicago, 1897. Stone-Swallowing by Seals. Unusual Twilight Phenomena Over Ethiopia. MacFarlane's Bear: Hybrid or Freak?* He used the clippings as bookmarks, stuffed them in envelopes, and finally began pasting them into spiral notebooks, organized by topic. *Spontaneous Combustion in Non-Human Species. Does the Sun Have a Seldom-Seen Companion Star?* Even the most unscientific, self-involved person would find these stories fascinating, he thought. PA Girl could say whatever she liked, he knew he was not, at his core, boring.

After graduation he stayed on at the labs, occasionally

moonlighting selling algae as a nutritional supplement door to door (RIDE THE GREEN WAVE TO FREEDOM!, an indestructible bumper sticker on his Toyota still read), but his anomaly collection had taken on a life of its own, growing even when he neglected it. Clippings came to him unsolicited from around the country and world, from the most distant of acquaintances—though he could not recall having mentioned his hobby to so many people. He supposed the urge to collect accounts of freak occurrences was primal and universal, but people seemed especially eager for *him* to do it, including little notes with their clippings like "This made me think of you!" and "Your kind of thing!"

Of course, much of what they sent him did not constitute legitimate anomalies. Most items had logical explanations, easily attributable to the laws of nature and physics. Mexican Wolf-Boy, for example, had curiosity value but was not an anomaly because genetic mutation was a known process. If a story was completely unsubstantiated he couldn't use it either—anyone could claim to see their dead grandmother floating at the foot of their bed. He wasn't interested in proving the existence of the paranormal, or disproving it. He just wanted to create a place, a safe shelter, like an orphanage, for all the data science couldn't, or wouldn't, explain, and thus labeled unusable, unimportant.

He self-published the first volume using a press he found listed in the back of *Popular Astronomy* and ran a classified to sell the book mail-order, though he sent complimentary copies to his friends and family. *Finally, someone to follow in Donny's footsteps, ha ha,* his mother wrote back to him, referring to her late great-uncle, who at seventy-five had gotten a watch tattooed on his wrist to symbolize the meaninglessness of time and then spent his retirement trying to invent a perpetual-motion machine. The anomalist remembered visiting Donny's house as a child and seeing one of the prototypes sitting dusty and motionless in a corner of the garage—a nondescript boxlike device resembling a stereo speaker.

But the *Encyclopedia* wasn't sitting in a garage, it was selling, enough to pay for groceries and let him cut back his lab assignments, and to attract the attention of a small publishing house who wanted to put out Volumes II and III. He could not have put his finger on the single moment, the turning point when the project morphed from hobby into full-time job, but he found himself strangely relieved that it had. Leaving the house was overrated anyway, he thought. Too much travel always made him feel he was missing or forgetting something.

PA Girl had been right in one prediction: He could never have committed himself to a single discipline long enough to make it as a marine biologist, a research pioneer, doing the kind of specialized, significant work that changed lives and the environment and history. *To look very closely at a certain object,* he remembered from some art class he'd been required to take, *means you are looking away from many other objects.* He could never turn away from the messy multitude of everything—he was a collector.

Secretly, and then with increasing confidence as he completed each new volume, he believed the *Encyclopedia* would one day come to be seen as seminal, significant as any newly discovered species or element or cure. Hadn't mainstream science scoffed at continental drift, quantum physics, only to canonize them a few years later? In future times his collection would stand, testimony to all that couldn't be fitted easily into somebody's theory of how the world worked. He would leave the discoveries to others, but some of these, he believed, would arise and take shape, like the first stirrings of life itself, from the pages of data he was slowly amassing.

By the time he was thirty he had published the first seven volumes, covering the disciplines of biology, geology, physics, astronomy, archeology, psychology, and mathematics; now he worked by subcategory and sub-subcategory for the auxiliary volumes: *Anomalous Hydrological Phenomena. Auditory Hallucinations. Unexplained Detonations, Possibly Seismic.* There was no end to the oddball, ragtag data cast off by science, calling out for his attention. And as long as he was breathing, no anomaly would spin off into oblivion, left to float in obscurity like a dead star or an unseen meteor. He'd be there to catch them all, give them their proper due.

The Buffalo

When he was five he got his head stuck in a fence at the Imagination Station, a scenic overlook on the edge of a Florida state preserve, where one could view alligators and sandhill cranes and bison, *if you're in the right place at the right time,* a carved plaque read. That phrase excited him— it sounded like a challenge or the rules to a mysterious game. He was on vacation from the snowy north with his family, his first time in Florida, overstimulated by the blitz of color and light, the prehistoric trees and rotting-fruit smell everywhere. Instead of waiting his turn to be held up, he pushed his head between two aluminum fence poles, but all he saw was green, flat as a game board. Oversized insects looped down in front of his face, but no buffalo appeared. And he was stuck.

A long time passed, but he didn't cry. His mother took his brothers away to get sandwiches and his father stayed with him, neither of them saying much. His mother returned and pushed wads of Arby's roast beef into his mouth. Other grown-ups came and went; different hands folded his neck and shoulders this way and that. He couldn't see their faces, but he answered their questions politely. His scalp grew hot and made him sleepy, but he stayed awake in case a buffalo appeared. This might not be the right place, he thought, but he was bound to get the right time, stuck here for so long. It made a lot more sense to wait in one place for a whole day or year or however long it took for that place's right time to come along, he thought, than to run randomly, frantically, from place to place, diminishing your chances at each of them. That would just be stupid.

Finally the man with the special saw arrived. The man lowered the long serrated blade before his eyes so he could see it—and then he began to cry. *Don't worry, he's only going to saw* near *your head,* his mother said. *Close your eyes, it'll be over in a minute.* But he kept them open. He wasn't really crying because of the saw, anyway, but because of the sudden, certain realization that if he shut his eyes, even for an instant, the buffalo would come out—he was sure of it. He understood everything: He could keep his eyes open and the buffalo wouldn't appear, or close them and it would. The buffalo knew exactly what it was doing, he thought, knew how to win every time. He kept his eyes open. No buffalo.

And, sure enough, after they finally got him free and checked him over, thanked and paid the man with the saw and loaded themselves back into the station wagon and pulled back onto the highway, he watched the prairie through the back window, and just before they rounded the first curve he saw it: the black crescent edge of a huge blunt shape, nosing slowly out of the underbrush, victorious.

His Assistant
Maybe he'd gone to school in Florida and then remained all these years just to try to get another glimpse of that buffalo. Unconsciously, that is. Consciously, he hadn't thought about

the buffalo for ages until Maggie, his assistant, asked him about his childhood.

It was odd—if someone else had asked him, or if she had asked in a different way, he would have been annoyed. PA Girl had always wanted to analyze everyone's childhood. But Maggie was so matter-of-fact and businesslike, her fingers ticking away at her keyboard, inputting copyright permissions, her voice nearly without inflection . . . and besides, there was just something about her that made him want to talk, tell her things about himself. Very odd.

He'd hired her part-time to help answer correspondence, which had increased exponentially with every volume, but lately she stayed into the evenings, working on his web site. She'd been the first to answer the notice he'd posted at the university, a graduate student in computer science, twenty-five or -six, he guessed—not so much younger than himself, though why should he care?—lugging phonebook-sized texts with titles like *Revolutions in Interfacing* and *Information Encryption and Retrieval* in a pink Hello Kitty backpack.

It was her idea, after only a couple days on the job, to set up Anomalies.com—"to expedite and consolidate all your advertising, correspondence, and documentation in one venue," she said—and without too much deliberation, he agreed. For some reason, she inspired his confidence. Maybe because he had no idea what she was talking about, or because she seemed to lack some essential feminine element. She wore a dress every day and some kind of strawberry perfume, and had a whole battery of girlish gestures, twiddling her mismatched earrings or stretching her plastic bracelets over her wrists as she spoke—but she just didn't seem capable of flightiness, the unpredictable surges and bursts of emotion his girlfriends had all sooner or later surrendered to and even seemed to celebrate, like glorious holidays from rationality. Maybe she was gay. But no, she'd said something about a boyfriend, he thought. Anyway, when she was frowning at her computer monitor she gave off a grim, unrelenting energy he could not recall ever having witnessed in a woman, or, for that matter, anyone.

"Did you have a good childhood?" she asked, monotone, eyes on the screen. She asked it in the same way she might ask if he'd had a nice lunch.

"Yeah," he rasped, then cleared his throat—he hadn't spoken in two or three hours. He gazed out at his overgrown yard, through the humid grime of Florida summer caked like agar on the picture window, primordial

microscopic life forms probably coming into existence before his eyes. Even so, the sunset was lovely, broad green
and pink rays. *That buffalo,* he suddenly remembered. He
told Maggie the story.

"Oh, I've been there," she said. "My kids love that place.
Why don't you go back sometime? It's only a couple hours
from here. I'm sure you'll see one if you just keep going.
We've seen them a few times."

He was stunned. It had never occurred to him to go back
to the Imagination Station. He'd had no idea it was so close,
or even still existed, had ever existed, except in his memory.
She had kids? They'd seen a buffalo?

She was looking at him in her level way. Her mouth was
small and crooked, like an unfinished line on a drawing.
"How many kids?" he managed to say.

"Two. Four and five and a half. I share custody with my
ex." She sounded almost apologetic. At the mention of her
ex, he suddenly could breathe again.

"In fact," she went on, "I was thinking, if you needed
someone to work on your yard? I don't know if you're interested, but he's a professional landscaper. And he does
carpentry on the side—he can build a shed in forty-five
minutes. If you're interested."

He couldn't imagine what he'd need a shed for, but he was fiercely curious all of a sudden to see this guy put one up in forty-five minutes, and he could tell she was worried she'd offended him. His yard was a mess, but he preferred it that way: naturalists sneered at frequent mowing and weed control. "Sure, I'll take a shed," he said.

"Also, would it be okay if I moved in with you?" she said.

He often thought one of the great advantages of living as he did, not wasting any time thinking or talking about or trying to identify your emotions, was that unlike most people, you didn't have to suffer through long periods of unrequited desire, the roller coaster between determination and doubt, the exhausting internal debate, like a TV channel you could never turn off, over whether to make a move or wait. Instead, what often occurred, if you were sufficiently out of touch with your feelings, was that, miraculously, at the very moment you finally realized you wanted something, had been wanting it for weeks or even months without ever recognizing it, it came to you.

She was still speaking, telling a convoluted story involving her ex-sister-in-law and her Pell grant and a security deposit that wasn't going to be returned to her because of something her daughter had done to a toilet. "Fine," he interrupted. "What do you want to pay, two hundred a month? Is that too much? I'll just take it out of your paycheck, if that's easier. Would it just be you, or your kids also? Do you have a boyfriend?" He threw the question in, a stowaway, an item sneaked into Mom's grocery cart, hoping she wouldn't notice.

"No, the thing is," she said, then stopped. "Look, *thanks*. This is perfect, I can walk to school from here. The kids would need to stay here three days a week, though."

"Fine, fine," he said. No boyfriend—she could move in dinosaurs for all he cared.

"The thing is," she said, "would it be possible to do, like, a month-to-month? Because I might be getting back together with my ex. I mean, we're working on it, who knows?"

"Fine," he said.

She was smiling right at him, lopsided and blinding, more binding than a signature. Too late to get out of it. Getting back together with her ex—of course she was. What had he been thinking? The mass and gravity of all her attachments, her relationships and obligations, made a small palpable atmosphere, like that of a planet, around her person. How foolish to think he could penetrate it. Her hair, he noticed now, curved in a sleek barrier around her face, a familiar black crescent—why hadn't he noticed it before? How stupid, to have thought he was getting away with something, getting her so easily, as if anyone ever really put anything over on the universe, tricked the buffalo, won.

The following weekend he watched her ex, who had the scrubbed, sunny features and resourceful bearing of a camp counselor, help unload and carry in her few cartons and pieces of furniture and the children's thousand toys, and then do his thing, clambering over a pile of plywood in the anomalist's yard like some nest-building creature, boards in both hands, then standing triumphant on the roof when it was done, Maggie applauding from the mold-blackened deck where she sat sipping Hawaiian Punch with the impossibly beautiful children, *Erik and Rosabelle*—their names charged and faintly painful to the anomalist's ear, like the names of remote, mythological islands. He watched her sling her pink backpack up onto her shoulders every morning, and when she was gone he stood in the hall outside the guest bathroom, smelling her shampoo and picking the kids' He-Man Band-Aids off the soles of his feet. He saved the notes she slipped under his office door when she borrowed his car: *Chuck E. Cheese 2-for-1 nite,* and, *I'm out of Skintimate.*

Idiot. Really, how ignorant could a grown-up person be—to have believed, even for a moment, that he could escape pain, detour around desire. There were no shortcuts. You didn't even need to leave your house to know that much.

Plane Takes Off Without Pilot, Flies for Two Hours

Every now and then the anomalist came across an item that was not an anomaly per se but which sparked his attention, stayed in his mind even after he had rejected it for inclusion in the *Encyclopedia.* Not the stuff the zealots and *X-Files* freaks sent him, apparitions and miracles, modern-day fertility statues and Virgin-shaped water stains, so familiar they scarcely seemed miraculous anymore. Rather, he found himself enchanted with examples of simple human error, mundane malfunctions and mechanical glitches. The sheer variety of things that could and did go wrong in the world never failed to surprise and strangely comfort him.

The plane got a two-paragraph mention in the local paper's "Around the Nation" section, and he quickly ruled it nonanomalous: An Ohio pilot got out to check the propeller on his single-engine and started the motor by mistake. The empty plane taxied, took off, "circled the area for about five minutes before heading northeast," the paper said, and eventually crashed in a cabbage field ninety miles away, injuring no one. An accident, wholly explainable.

Still, he wished he could have been there to see it. The pilot's face the moment he realized what was happening. The great white-and-silver shape speeding out of reach, graceful and pointy-nosed as a runaway greyhound. And *whoosh,* like magic, lift-off, escape! The ascent into air, triumphant hum, pure force, what did it need people for?

Children

The anomalist's house was filled with children. He wasn't sure how many, or how it had happened, exactly, but they were everywhere, sprawled on the floor or hiding, hunched and flattened, under furniture, hurling themselves through sprays of water in the yard and hanging upside down in his trees, rocketing up and down the hallway outside his closed office door. He could identify some of them: Aimee from Baby Aerobics, Lysander from day care, three sequin-costumed girls Maggie claimed were her nieces, an overweight girl in a poodle skirt who didn't seem to know any of the other children though she was a frequent visitor, an indeterminate number of school-age kids from the neighborhood, all of whom who seemed completely familiar with and comfortable in his kitchen—the other day one of them had shown him how to use his built-in can opener—and the twins, solemn, diapered Indian-looking boys whose connection to Maggie he could never keep straight, though they seemed ever more frequently to be in her care.

At night, six or twelve of them might be camped in bags on the deck or in the forty-five-minute shed—he certainly had no use for it, himself—or in Maggie's room, or in the extra bedroom she had recently stripped and repapered. ("The violets were running the room," she told him. "Fine," he said, "they were here when I bought the house, I never liked them, do whatever you want." He couldn't quite appreciate how her sponge-painted border was an improvement, but he didn't care, as long as she knew he hadn't chosen the violets.) The house was growing a self-perpetuating layer of detritus, like the tangle of bromeliad and palmetto scrub taking over his yard—only this consisted of stickers, glitter, jigsaw pieces, Barbie torsos, hamster turds, crackers with the salt sucked off, pages ripped from picture books, paper towels sodden with juice and blood. He'd thought of himself as someone who respected messiness, but now he modified that: he respected plurality, complexity, inclusion. He liked order. Categories, taxonomy.

He was adept at shutting out distractions, but children's noise, he decided, was not like regular noise. It was not the quantity but the quality that was so different—the abruptness and complete unpredictability, how the house went from calm to chaos in two seconds without warning or obvious cause, shrieks boiling up out of pure silence as though disaster bulged behind every peaceful moment, held back by the flimsiest of membranes. The noise of children was not a subset of the functional hum of society, he thought, but something separate and primitive, *anomalous,* the sound track of anarchy itself, Armageddon, the end of the world.

Okay, that was an exaggeration, but his nerves were skinned, and for the first time, he was behind deadline on a book—*Volume XI, Unexplained Migratory Behavior in Mammals. Sheep panics,* he typed, teeth clenched, trying to ignore a voice in the yard screaming, "I'm doing the same thing Kristin is!" To his knowledge, none of the children living at his house were named Kristin. *Granted, sheep panics do not display the duration or directional discipline of lemming migrations,* he wrote. *Sheep panics, then, might not represent a true anomaly, but rather a reaction to some climatic stimulus, such as a meteoric fireball.* Someone kick-knocked, sneaker-toed, on his office door, then pushed it open before he could answer. He swiveled his chair, ready to yell, but it was Rosabelle, holding up by the armpits a dwarf rabbit on whose mouth red lipstick had been applied. The rabbit looked at him with no expression.

"What's its name?" he heard himself asking.

"Zsa Zsa Zsa Zsa Gabor," Rosabelle said. She looked wildly proud, hopeful, thrilled. Her small face was as serious and luminous as her mother's, asymmetrical and out-of-place pale in Florida.

"You mean Zsa Zsa Gabor," he said.

"No, Z-S-A, Z-S-A, that's how it's spelled. Zsa, Zsa, Zsa, Zsa, Gabor," she said.

"Z-S-A-Z-S-A spells Zsa Zsa," he said.

"No, it spells Zsa Zsa Zsa Zsa," she said.

"Where's your mom? Would you please go get her so I can talk to her?"

"She's not here," Rosabelle said. "She went to see the human racehorse lady."

"Damn it," he said. Hakeem, his old algae-selling buddy,

had warned him about this when Maggie moved in. *Single mom, uh-oh, you better beware, my friend! Why can't you get a crush on one of these, there's only 30,000 of 'em,* Hakeem shouted, gesturing gleefully at the river of big-haired, short-shorted coeds biking and jogging along on either side of them as they drove through town on Nickel Beer Night. None of them looked anything like Maggie, the anomalist thought, and not just because they were mostly blond, and tanned—they didn't take up space in the same way she did. Their matter seemed less dense. *You're gonna be Mr. Mom, buddy, I'm telling you, that's what they all want,* Hakeem hammered. Of course Hakeem was right, the anomalist saw now. She was taking advantage of him. It wouldn't have bothered him so much, he knew, if he weren't in love with her. He remembered a paperback about assertiveness PA Girl was always trying to get him to read, called *How to Say the Second "No."* He had refused, a little smugly, thus proving he had no problem asserting himself. Now he wished he had read it.

"Is anyone here?" he asked Rosabelle.

"Yeah," she said. "Everyone's here."

"All right, look, I'll come out there in a minute, but you have to leave me alone right now, okay?" he said. "I'm trying to do something important."

"Okay," Rosabelle said. She dropped the bunny down so its hind feet touched the floor, then walked it slowly out of the room. "I'm doing something important," he heard her say to somebody, or nobody, in the hall.

"Your two and your two only," he told Maggie, a couple nights later. He firmed his voice, barrierlike, against the jittering in his stomach. She sat across from him in a booth at the Happy Family Restaurant, the Chinese place the kids loved, formerly a Howard Johnson, now all black-and-red chipped lacquer, oil-stained place mats and misspelled menu items—but at least they were alone, for once. Erik and Rosabelle were with Shed Boy, nieces and neighbors returned to their families, twins gone back to wherever they came from. "Twenty-four-hour supervision, you or a sitter, no teenagers, no sleepovers, if more than two friends visit everyone goes to the playground. What else? No more pets. They can keep the ones they have, but no new ones. Except fish. Fish are okay."

He had been talking to his lap, his flatware, but now, finally looking up at her lovely, washed-out, backlit silhouette, he got the physical sensation of looking into a fire, the faint pressure of heavier-than-normal air rolling across the table, warming his face into a squint. He waited, held his breath.

"You're right," she said. "I'll move out."

"No!" he said.

"No, it's no problem," she said.

"Where?"

"Back in with Shed Boy," she said.

When had she started calling him that? He was sure—well, pretty sure—he had never said it aloud. She looked shaken, something moving through her impassive features, a ripple in her normal cloaked steadiness.

"No," he said. He saw himself reaching across for her wrist, her warm cheap beads beneath his fingers, a handcuff, she couldn't go so easily, didn't she care? "No." Why was it whenever he started speaking he could only seem to say the same thing over and over? "I don't want you to move out, I want you to stay," he said. "I mean, with me." His ears roared, maybe the MSG. He had thought about this moment, imagined and planned it, but now it was hopelessly tangled in the other moment, like socks in a drawer, indistinguishable, inextricable, a mess.

But she wasn't pulling away—she was holding on to his hand, as if they'd touched every day, or ever, in the months they'd lived together, her open, weary face moving and shocking as a rare bird in his yard, someone's escaped exotic pet, the bright incongruous flash of beauty in the trees. "I'd like to stay," she said. "With you." When he didn't immediately speak, she added, "At least until finals, do you mind?"

It was that easy. He felt dizzy, knocked off-balance by the lack of resistance—like the time he opened his office door and Erik, who had been leaning hard against it, fell into the room. All he'd had to do was ask. What was it he'd had against relationships again?

To look very closely at a certain object means you are looking away from many other objects, he remembered, his arm over her in bed, no she could not get up to go to the bathroom, did she mind?—okay, fine, but make it quick. Even with her out of the room, he felt her beside him, unwavering, a steady current in the dark. The lamp of her sweet white face, damp and determined and literal. So easily, obviously, his—had he gotten her just by looking closely, looking away from everything else?

"Why didn't you say something months ago?" she'd asked, naked and rational in his arms. "I mean, if you felt this way."

"I didn't have a choice, did I?" he said. "I suppose I've always thought if you really wanted something you shouldn't ask for it. I don't know why. I suppose I've always thought I had no choice."

"Well, I do understand that," she said. "I never wanted to watch all those kids—half of them I barely know. I just couldn't say no when someone asked me to baby-sit, for some reason. Like I owed them, or something—complete strangers. Really, it's ridiculous, I mean, those aren't even my nieces."

"Who are the twins again?" he asked now, sleepily, as she returned to him, creaking across the room, without turning on the light, and back into the mattress, into the L of his outstretched arm.

"Well, technically they're not U.S. citizens," she began, but he drifted off and missed the rest of what she said. Eyes closed, he felt them falling, spinning off together into space, *Ride the green wave to freedom,* their own glittery gold-hazed atmosphere swirling behind them like the tail of a comet: sparks, stones, sheep, stars, Barbies, pizzas, planets, rabbits . . . all without leaving the house.

The Preface

Whenever the anomalist got depressed, he worked on the Preface. He'd started it in response to his critics, the hate

mail—and now e-mail—he received from creationists and
Darwinists alike, paranormal enthusiasts and skeptics. *The
Lord shows no mercy towards those who attempt to explain away His miracles.* And from the other side: *You're
selling nothing but voodoo science, snake oil — you give science a bad name!* The debunkers were worse than the
fanatics, more focused and articulate in their attacks. A professor of physics had devoted an entire chapter to the anomalist in his best-selling book, *Science or Scam?* A blurb on
the back read, *Professor Haney does more than debunk, he
crucifies, and the result is huge fun!*

The anomalist had explained in his Introduction to the
Encyclopedia's first volume that his intention was to con-
tribute to science, not corrupt it—but clearly that wasn't
enough. He needed something longer and more inspira-
tional, a philosophical mission statement, which when per-
fected could serve as the Preface for every volume, uniting
and uplifting the series, doing justice to it not only as a navi-
gable group of reference texts, but as a single unimpeach-
able body of dazzling data.

There was no hurry to finish the Preface, which was now
running upward of twenty pages, as it couldn't be ap-
pended, his publisher warned, until the *Encyclopedia* was

complete and the existing volumes all went into their second printing. But still, working on it never failed to make him feel better. *It is as important to recognize what is* not *known as to recognize what is known,* he wrote. *I visualize the day when every person—student, scientist, or layman—has ready access to a fully indexed shelf of volumes identical to the one you hold in your hand today—a catalogue of all that cannot be explained.* The anomalist considered working on the unpublishable Preface his one concession to irrationality.

Only, lately, like a drug to which he'd built up tolerance, it wasn't helping. The debunkers didn't rattle him so much anymore—he even felt a growing fondness for them, their reassuringly familiar rhetoric, their unswayable position in the firmament, which only served to confirm his own. Instead, he found himself undone, increasingly, by what seemed like nothing—by moments. Not the moments that made up his days with Maggie and the kids, happier days than he'd hoped or planned for, but other moments that didn't belong to him, or his life, yet were in it. When Shed Boy came to drop off a cardigan or thermos cap the kids forgot, for instance, and Maggie stood chatting with him in the driveway, dark and light heads tilted casually close together, their bond an easy open secret in the sunlight. Or Erik's almost painfully bright face when he asked Maggie a question—a glow so like his father's, though on Erik, the anomalist thought, the brightness was *appropriate,* not precious and obscene. But not his to appreciate, not fully. And the shed. Its garish, prefab, vinyl-sided bulk, ruining the view out his office window. An artificial, chemical, gray-tinged green that managed not to match any of the eight million shades of moss and grass and flower in the yard.

One afternoon he went out and looked at it up close, the first time he'd done so since the day it was built, when he was required to inspect and praise Shed Boy's efforts. It was a graceless thing, he thought now, no promise, all practicality. The opposite of a perpetual-motion machine, even a defunct one. Even the kids had grown tired of it months ago, no longer used it for sleepovers. He peeked inside—a length of leaky hose, a broken-handled bucket containing a tennis ball. He ran his palm over the siding, put his face up to a panel and sniffed it: no smell. All man-made. For a second, he actually felt sorry for it, or for someone, he couldn't say who. But that was ridiculous—why feel sorry for an inanimate object?

No one else was home.

How hard could it be to tear down a shed? A little hard, it turned out, but not very. He got a crowbar from the garage, but he barely needed it once he'd pried away the corrugated roof and knocked the floor off its cinder-block foundation. The whole thing was only six by eight, corners designed to snap together—and apart—like a toy. The process took on a kind of momentum, getting quicker as he went: the less of it there was, the easier it was to destroy. He wasn't even sweating much. And though it might have wished to, the shed could give him no splinters.

When he was done, he gathered up the trove of Wiffle balls and Legos and doll limbs the demolition had uncovered, ran them under the spigot on the side of the house, and spread them on the deck to dry. The kids would be happy about that.

Then he carried the pieces of the shed around front and stacked them at the curb for pickup, wiped his hands on his jeans, and looked at his watch: forty-eight minutes. Rosabelle and a friend were coming up the street from the park, he saw, dragging Beanie Babies on yarn leashes, Rosabelle occasionally whipping hers in circles over her head like a lasso. Maggie would be back from class any minute.

He went inside, showered, and shut himself in his office, swiveling his chair away from the window. He felt better already, scrolling down the stanzas on his screen. *Sudden blanching of the hair, a complex phenomenon about which we know next to nothing. Deaf people able to dream noise.* Whatever she did, whatever part of her heart he could not hope to reach, whatever hurts lurked ahead for him like practical jokes, Candid Camera, *Ha ha, it was Shed Boy I loved all along*—whatever happened, his anomalies would not desert him. He envisioned them his children, himself the father, for once, the tireless provider who would never let them come to harm.

From outside came ether-pitched squeals of recognition. And Maggie's low voice: "Hmmm, that's very interesting."

He clicked open the Preface and began to type. *Will this Encyclopedia revolutionize science? Probably not in my lifetime—too many anomalies, not enough time. There is much work still to be done. The end is not even in sight . . .*

The Buffalo

It was almost dark when they got to the Imagination Station, sunset a watery late-November yellow on either side of the highway. There was a new fence, he noticed right away, wide-spaced horizontal wooden slats.

"You know, buffalo are the only animals who don't get cancer," he told the kids as they piled out. Rosabelle ran ahead, red sneakers flashing under the lanterns just flickering on around the parking area. Maggie zipped up Erik's windbreaker, then let him loose.

When they caught up to the kids he thought at first there must be no buffalo, because Rosabelle had her back to the overlook, and was watching a moth going crazy under a lantern, spinning a tight, mad orbit around a vertical post of the fence. "That looks like fun," she said.

Then Maggie touched his shoulder, said, "Shh," and pointed.

They looked different than he'd imagined, not the sinister, tricky shape he remembered, but lopsided and guileless, top-heavy and incongruous and unbalanced-looking, yet still graceful somehow, like great black pianos gliding through the grass. They moved idly, in no hurry, three, five, eight, out into the open, making no sound.

"That's them all right," Erik whispered.

He'd thought the children might be bored, having come here so many times already, but when he turned around the boy was looking at him expectantly, arms held straight over his head, waiting to be lifted up.

NIPPLE

IN THE CAFETERIA fourth period Lori said she had her
Uncle Bert's nipple in an envelope. We were all like, What
are you talking about, and she was like, I'm not kidding, his
nipple fell off and I got it and he doesn't even know I have
it. We were all like, screaming, except Meghan, who was
like, Right, I'm sure your own nipple falls off and you don't
even notice. Lori was like, It's in my locker, I'd be delighted
to show you if you don't believe me, and Meghan was like,
Woo, *delighted*, well excuse me, Miss Manners, why don't
you send out embroidered invitations and hold a ceremony?
Then she stood up and left, because she had to make up

dissecting a fetal pig from when she had mono. Lori was like, What's her problem.

The rest of us were like, Just ignore her, so how did you get his nipple? And Lori goes, I found it in the shower, stuck in the drain thing, I almost stepped on it. Andrea was like, In five seconds I'm going to throw up. I was like, How do you know that's what it is, how do you know it's not a scab, or something, like, else? And Lori was like, Well, he visits every year from Canada and he always walks around without his shirt on, 'cause in the morning he does, like, the Canadian Air Force exercises or something, so every year I've been like *noticing* that his one nipple looks like it's hanging on a thread. It wasn't like bleeding or anything, it was just like, not *attached* all the way. The other one was fine, but that one was like, falling off. I've been waiting for it to fall off for like, three years.

Why was it like that, I asked her. Was he born with it that way or did something happen? Did he get it caught in something, like a zipper or a stapler or something?

Andrea stood up and was like, Excuse me, I am literally going to throw up now. We watched her leave, but she was heading toward the vending machines, not the bathrooms. She's like in love with Junior Mints. Lori was like, I have no idea how it got that way but I knew it was going to fall off eventually.

All of a sudden, Michelle was like, Wait, oh my God, remember, weren't you telling us that time about how your uncle got hit by lightning on a totally clear day playing horseshoes at a wedding and how now he's thirsty all the time and he never gets cold and he knows stuff before it happens? Well, maybe it happened when the lightning hit him, maybe it hit him exactly on his nipple, or even if it hit him on his back, wouldn't that be strong enough to make his nipple fall off?

But Lori said no, that was her other uncle. Michelle was like, Oh. Then she stood up and said she had to go because she had a conference with Mr. Stirnad, the new guidance counselor who's like never brushed his teeth in his life, and we were like, Bye, don't forget your gas mask.

So then it was just me and Lori sitting there, waiting for the bell to ring, and I was like, So are you going to mail it to him in Canada? And Lori just looked at me like, *Okaayy*, and I was like, *What?* And she goes, *Mail* it to him? Are you feeling okay? And I was like, Well you said you put it in an envelope, so I just figured you were going to send it to him.

She just gave me this total look and was like, I don't

think so—are you, like, mental? Then he'd know I had it, and he'd think I, like, *wanted* it or something. God, Jenny, I can't even believe you just said that! Plus, it's not that kind of envelope, it's one of those little wax-paper ones from the orthodontist, you know, that your rubber bands come in? God, though, Jenny, I still can't believe you just said that. I swear, sometimes I think you are seriously mental. She sat there staring at me with her mouth open.

I was like, Well excuse me for living on planet Earth— but I didn't say anything. I was just like, whatever. Because that's the whole thing about Lori, she never lets anything drop. It's just like the nipple, it's like, no matter how small or totally irrelevant a thing is, if she's there, forget it, she'll get ahold of it somehow, and keep bringing it up for all eternity. She's like if you had to look into one of those lit-up Revlon magnifying mirrors that make your face look like a mountainous terrain, for like twenty-four hours a day.

And, incidentally, I know I'm not the only person who feels that way, because for like six months after that, every time Meghan passed Lori in the hall, she'd wave her fingers in Lori's face like she was doing voodoo or trying to hyp-

notize her or something, and go, *Woo, delighted, delighted.*
So Lori basically stopped talking to Meghan altogether, but
the whole thing about Meghan is that ever since the whole
thing with the minister at her church hitting on her, she
doesn't exactly care.

THE HUMAN SIDE OF INSTRUMENTAL TRANSCOMMUNICATION

GREETINGS, AND WELCOME to the third annual Conference of the Instrumental Transcommunication Network. Special welcome to those organizations joining us this year for the first time: the Engineering Anomalies Research Society (EARS), the Electromagnetic Aberrations Research Society (also EARS), the Tinnitus Family, and Chronic Pain Anonymous. We are delighted to see such a large turnout—surely our growing numbers indicate that the validity of instrumental transcommunication is becoming apparent to even our most outspoken critics.

I would now like to share some thoughts about the

meaning of this year's conference theme, "The Human Side of Instrumental Transcommunication." For myself, founder of the Instrumental Transcommunication Network, the answer to the question "Why use tape recorders, televisions, and computers to attempt to communicate interdimensionally with spirit beings?" has always been a highly personal one.

My involvement in the field began four years ago in St. Augustine, Florida, where I was vacationing with my wife and son, Nathan—who at that time was the only person in our family with a particular interest in recording equipment. Then seven years old, he already owned a dozen miniature tape recorders, and more cassettes than crayons. When he was only a baby he had discovered my wife's little Panasonic portable from her journalism school days, digging it out of a box in the basement and screaming when we tried to pry it away. Thereafter, we bought tape recorders for him wherever we saw them, at thrift stores, flea markets, garage sales we happened to pass. They were cheap, we reasoned, too big to swallow, and Nathan couldn't seem to get enough of them—he carried them around like pet hamsters and wouldn't sleep without one or two in his bed. On his first day of kindergarten an entire wing of his school had to be evacuated when the tape recorder he kept in his windbreaker got stuck on fast-forward in the coatroom and was believed to be a ticking bomb.

He just had a way with those little machines. He could rewind or fast-forward any cassette tape to the exact spot he wanted on the first try, without using the counter device, and on long car trips my wife and I took turns requesting songs from the middles of tapes to keep him busy. He would sit on the floor under the dashboard and put his ear up next to the tape deck like a safecracker, and then his whole face would light up as though someone had flipped a switch behind it when he hit the right spot, pressed the play button, and my wife's favorite song came on once again, perfectly cued to the beginning. He never missed, and, like any good magician, he never told his secrets.

Interestingly, though, despite his love for junky cassette players, Nathan didn't care at all for the brand-new Walkman my wife's mother bought him. His real love, we discovered, was for making tapes, not listening to them, so we allowed him to make as many as he wanted. He recorded himself talking in different voices, acting out dramas full of coyotes, opera singers, helicopters, Mack trucks, nuclear emergency alert sirens, hives of angry bees. In his stories people had frequent arguments, and there were many slamming doors, much shouting to be let in or out.

He was so enthusiastic about his sound effects that he tended to neglect things like plot and logic, jumping from one sensational noise to another without explanation, rushing through dialogue and mixing up his voices so that half the time we couldn't understand what any of his characters were saying, or even what was going on. "You'll have to slow down and enunciate," my wife, ever the good editor, would tell him, "because whatever you just said there is not a word." But Nathan paid no heed. "If it's not a word," he argued, "then how come I just said it?"

Of course, he could not have understood how meaningful that offhand remark would come to be, to so many of us. He was saying, of course, that *the act of communication is of greater significance than the means used to achieve it.* Who among us today has not felt deeply that very sentiment? But I digress.

On our trip to St. Augustine, I will always remember, Nathan wished for three things: to visit a Spanish war fort, to find and bring home an unbroken sand dollar, and to get the hotel maid to talk into his tape recorder. This was his first stay in a hotel since he was a baby, and he grew very excited when we explained to him that a lady was going to come into our room while we weren't there and make our beds and leave clean towels for us. "A lady we know?" he asked, and when we told him no, a strange lady, he concluded it was the tooth fairy, or someone just like her, perhaps her friend. This was where they probably lived, he said —in Florida. We tried to explain the truth without letting on that the tooth fairy wasn't real, but Nathan only grew more certain in his belief. Every morning before we left the hotel room to go down to breakfast or the beach, he set up one of his tape recorders on the dresser with this note:

Dear cleaning lady,
Please press Play and Record at the same time and then read this message out loud, begin Here.

   Hello, this is the cleaning lady coming to you live from the hotel. Today will be hot and sunny. Now, back to you.

When you are done press Stop.

Unfortunately, the woman never responded. Every night when we returned to the room Nathan ran to the recorder, but it had never been touched, and he grew more disappointed every day. We had already photographed him waving down at us from the parapet of the war fort, and he had not one but several perfect specimens of sand dollars wrapped in Kleenex like cookies and tucked for safety in our suitcase pockets. Yet these successes seemed only to make him more frustrated, as if this were some fairy tale where he had to satisfy an angry king. "Why didn't she do it, why?" he cried to us, night after night. It was possible the cleaning lady didn't speak or read English, we told him, or, more likely, she didn't want to disturb the belongings of guests—or perhaps she never even saw the note, or realized it was intended for her.

Privately my wife and I discussed tracking this woman down and talking to her, or finding another hotel employee who would cooperate, or even disguising one of our voices and recording the message ourselves. We *had* written little notes to him from the tooth fairy, my wife said, and wasn't this the same thing? But in the end we decided it was best to leave the situation to chance. Since we knew the maid was a real person capable of responding, we wanted her message, should it come, to be genuine. My wife eventually came to question this decision, but, as all of us here today undoubtedly understand, in such a situation integrity cannot be compromised, regardless of how desperately our hearts might long for different outcomes to our experiments.

Consider the pioneers in our field: Dr. Konstantin Raudive, who made more than one hundred thousand separate recordings after hearing a single mysterious voice on a blank, brand-new tape; or Friedrich Juergenson, who abandoned his successful opera-singing career so he could investigate electronic voice phenomena full-time after some strange voices speaking Norwegian turned up on a tape on which he had recorded birdcalls. Falsifying results was never an option for these scientists, as it should never be for us.

Yet despite our faithfulness to the scientific method, we must not ignore the personal factor in these experiments —the human side of instrumental transcommunication. For the personal relevance of the message, when it finally comes, is often what establishes the message's authenticity. Those of you who have already received such messages report that the sender will often use, as a kind of password, a phrase or nickname or piece of information that only he and you, the recipient, could know. Who can forget the message our esteemed colleagues Meek and O'Neil received on their Spiricom device, in the unmistakable voice of the deceased electronics specialist with whom they had worked for years: "The problem is an impedance mismatch into the third resistor—try a 150-ohm half-watt resistor in parallel with a .0047 micro-farad ceramic capacitor." Or Dr. Raudive's own unexpected message from the other side, which came through one night at home on the clock radio of the researcher who had been tirelessly advancing Raudive's cause after his untimely death: "This is Konstantin Raudive. Stay on the station, tune in correctly. Here it is summer, always summer! Soon it will work everywhere!" It almost seems that the deceased senders of these messages answered the calls of the living, rather than vice versa, as is usually assumed.

In light of these considerations, I strongly contend that my wife and I were justified in our choice not to fake the maid's voice on Nathan's tape. We could not have known what was about to occur.

For those of you not familiar with my story, which was reprinted in last month's newsletter, the paramedics who so heroically attempted to revive my son gave his cause of death as "generalized childhood seizure," meaning he had stopped breathing before he went underwater, rather than afterward. My wife, who was swimming not far away at the time, agrees; otherwise, she says, he would certainly have splashed or kicked, or cried out for help. She maintains she certainly would have heard him. We did recover the tape recorder in a Ziploc bag that he was carrying so he could record underwater sounds, but he hadn't sealed the bag properly, the whole thing was water-logged, and the cassette yielded nothing.

It might have been restored, of course, but my wife allowed the bag and its contents to be thrown away at the hospital—an oversight which some of us might find difficult to comprehend, but again, how could she have known? At that time, I myself knew nothing about instrumental transcommunication, not even that it existed. I knew nothing of the hours of research already completed, the extraordinary messages already received, the elaborate devices created by scientists and by ordinary men, like myself.

It was later that evening that the first seeds, as they say, were planted. To get back to our hotel we had to go through St. Augustine's cobblestoned sidestreets, past the crowded displays of artisans; one fellow dressed as a blacksmith called out to us, "Smile! It can't be that bad!" The very quality of the day's light seemed different, smoky, like a film

stuck on one frame, the edges burning and closing in. When
we got back, my wife went into the bathroom and shut the
door. Our room still smelled cheerfully of bananas and Sea
& Ski. The TV was on, for some reason, muted and tuned
to the closed-circuit bulletin board. A message was running
across the bottom of the screen: *If you like what you are*
hearing, tune in 24 hours a day. . . . *If you like what you are*
hearing, tune in 24 hours a day. . . .

That's when I noticed the recorder on the dresser, the one
Nathan had left for the maid. It was black and silver and
shining in the TV's cold blue light. But there was something
off about it, I thought, as if it had been touched or moved
by someone. Not the way he'd left it. Then, like a punch in
the stomach: Of course! The maid's message! She would
have done it this time. *Of course.* I saw it all at once, in simple, clear progression, our lives laid out as in a comic strip,
with everything—not just each day of our vacation, each
day the maid had not responded, but each day of Nathan's
life, our lives, our parents' lives before ours—leading up to
this, this final square, this *joke.*

I had to hear it anyway. I pressed play and held my
breath because it suddenly seemed too noisy, not right, and
with my breath stopped I felt the air around me stop, the

molecules stop popping, everything stop moving, so I could hear this awful answer, this stupid woman speak the words my son had written for her, too late. Instead, there was silence. Then, ever so faintly, something else, something so small, so familiar it seemed to come from my own body— but it could not have. It was breathing—Nathan, breathing. I waited for him to speak, to begin one of his stories, but he just went on breathing, as if he were just sitting there, reading his Sesame Street book, or lying on the floor, battling with his action figures. But *breathing*.

My wife was in the bathroom with the door closed. And my son, my son who I knew was dead, was breathing in my ear.

LIKE A DJ, God plays the impossible for us. I cannot speak for others, but that was how it began for me, founder of the Instrumental Transcommunication Network. I did not mistake the sound on the tape that night for the aspirations of a ghost, a message from the other side—but when I heard it, I knew such things were possible.

My wife was not there to receive the message. Was that only a fluke? Had she not been in the bathroom at that moment, I wonder, would she have heard it, too? Or did she leave the room on purpose, following some premonition, practicing a kind of willful deafness, the selective hearing of parents? It is impossible to say. Later, I brought home books for her—*Phone Calls from the Dead*, *The Inaudible Made Audible* in the original German, every seminal text in the field—but she refused to look at any of them. I might as well have handed her a stack of *Playboys*.

At the time of our divorce, we catalogued Nathan's tapes and stored them in a safe-deposit box so that I could continue my research, and so that she could listen to them for what her lawyer called "sentimental reasons"—an accusation, apparently. *I* am not the sentimental one, is the implication, not *human*, she has said. Yet it is she who refuses to take her own son's call, a call I have no doubt he will make, is perhaps preparing to make this very moment. I am ready. Upstairs in my room in this hotel the most sensitive and sophisticated equipment available at this time—thanks to many of you here today—is in operation even as we speak, poised and ready to receive and safeguard the most tentative inquiry, the faintest nudge of sound.

We are not spoon-benders, I tell my wife, and others like her, not flimflammers, but scientists and engineers, scholars and teachers and builders, fathers, many of us, and mothers. We wait like any line of people at a pay phone: impatient, hopeful, polite. What will he say when he calls? We can only imagine. It may not sound like English—it may not be English. We still have much work to do in the areas of clarity and amplification. On a typical recording, "soulmate" sounds like "sailboat," "father" may be indistinguishable from "bother," "Nathan" might come through as "nothing."

Still, we wait. We listen like safecrackers, we listen like sleuths. We remember the words of those listeners who came before us, the brave ones who started this whole thing. *Stay on the station, tune in correctly. Here it is summer, always summer! Soon it will work everywhere!*

Four Squirrels

Four squirrels tangled together by a plastic grocery bag struggle as they move up a tree Tuesday afternoon in Fredericksburg, Va. They were caught and taken to a veterinarian who freed them.

—Associated Press photo caption

I.

ALL LARRY DOES is talk about how it'll be when he's free—free of *us*. He's got big plans, big plans, and if it weren't for us, nothing would stop him. Not rain-slick shingles nor the topmost branches of skinny pines, not bird-feeder baffles, boys with BB guns, fenced yards full of smart-ass house cats. *Nothing!* Larry shouts. He'd beat them all, if only he didn't have us, his three siblings, tied to his tail. He doesn't know about us, he says, but when the big day comes, he's outta here, *sayonara,* my way or the highway, see ya, wouldn't wanna be ya!

In his excitement, he bites the air and madly lashes his tail, jerking the rest of us out of whatever peace we might have been enjoying. "Sorry, sorry," he says, but his eyes glitter with hysteria. "The big day is coming," he mutters—he tries to hold it in, then gives up. "It's COMING!" Larry screams. "I can FEEL it!"

Felicia is unimpressed. As the only female, she frequently takes that position. She is just perceptibly larger than the rest of us, bigger-boned, and her fur is sleeker. And lately she has developed something of a smell about her, a coy, insinuating odor that emanates invisibly out over our heads. Not that it does her any good: no normal squirrel would get within twenty feet of us, she says, and she's right. Occasionally some unsuspecting, unfettered, regular squirrel happens into our yard and sees us moving miserably along in our broken-pinwheel fashion, a malfunctioning machine made of fur bumping its way up the side of a pine tree— and he bolts. Their terror is tangible and predictable, the same every time: the first jolt of shock, and then the quick-blooming cloud of comprehension, that whatever we are, whatever it is that happened to us, *could happen to them.* Then, *whoosh,* they're gone, out of the yard before we can say a word.

"I hate it when that happens," Felicia has taken to saying.

Paul, as usual, says nothing. What I can see of his face when Larry isn't bobbing up between us—one black eye, a twitch of whisker, sometimes a millimeter of mouth—appears thoughtful. Or perhaps sad. No, thoughtful. I try not to dwell on Paul. Paul's silence, and I think I speak for all of us here, has become worrisome.

I, Marv, try to take the large view. I remind Felicia that we don't horrify *everyone,* that the yard in which we live is populated by insects of every variety, not to mention the bland assemblies of oblivious pigeons, the sparrows and finches trying to make an honest living, the lizards who sit around all day inflating their throats and doing push-ups for no apparent reason and who, therefore, would have a lot of nerve calling us odd-looking, and the grackles and starlings who take themselves very seriously and are much too busy attending meetings and discussing policy to give us a second thought.

"That's great, Marv, thanks," Felicia says. "I'll go fuck a grackle." When she says "fuck," a long shudder, kind of an extended wince, runs through all our bodies—certainly her intention. I glance nervously at Paul, but his eye is dark and inscrutable, steady as ever. I try to remember the last time I heard him say something, but I can't. And yet I know he must have spoken in the past; why else would his silence now seem so disturbing?

Things can change, I tell Felicia. And I believe it—I've seen plants wilt overnight, rain boil up out of an empty sky. But what I don't say, though I'm sure Felicia suspects or simply knows it, in her way, is that I *can't* imagine it, can't picture the four of us separate—free. Yet when I listen to Larry's escalating lament, or look for more than a moment into the inky weirdness of Paul's eye, I think perhaps I'm fortunate.

The thing is, I can't remember a time preceding our current condition. It must have happened to us in the nest, that elevated womb of leaves and fluff and flowing milk. We weren't trying to go anywhere then, we surely didn't think of ourselves as separate beings, and we never strived for anything but to burrow closer, deeper into the heat of each other. When we did finally come down, we moved in a group, as if propelled by one motor; the plastic had apparently been a part of us for weeks. Sure, we had our individual urges, our lunges at this pinecone, that candy wrapper, but no matter what caught the eye, drew the heart, of one of us, there was always the pull of the others.

So why, now, should we imagine ourselves otherwise? Why invite heartbreak and disillusionment?

Larry reminds Felicia that octopuses can unscrew jars. "And they are solitary, territorial creatures," he says. He is quoting the yellowed shred of newspaper that's braided in with the bag around our tails. "In the Philippines," he adds hopefully, "they have knifeless surgery."

"Here we go," Felicia says, rolling her eyes.

"Lightning hit the governor's airplane," Larry tells her. "There *is* an orthodontist who requires no down payment. On the next *Springer,* 'We May Be Identical Twins but I Hate Your Guts!' The perfect lobster is coming! Fisher-Price Knows!" There used to be more for him to read, but rain has worn most of the print away, and Larry, of late, recites the fragments he remembers more frequently and frantically, as if these blurred words from some distant authority, words that have nothing to do with us, are his last hope.

Also, he has begun to talk in his sleep. He describes

things that aren't in the paper and that he can't have seen firsthand, sky-high towers and cavernous, crater-sized wells, burning cities and men carrying crosses, human babies speaking archaic languages. The refrain is always the same: *The day of change is drawing near.*

And then, a few nights ago, the final straw—an incident we could neither tolerate nor ignore. During a stretch of impossible, rainless heat, in the middle of a night so warm the birds thought it was day and kept singing idiotically past midnight, Larry tried to chew himself loose. Felicia felt it first, woke the rest of us up shrieking and twisting around to try and reach him. There was the deranged smell of blood coming up from where his mouth was fastened, on the lump of hair and bone and plastic that connected us. "OUCH!" someone screamed, and suddenly we were flipping through the air, out of the crook of the oak where we slept. We bounced twice against the bark and hit the ground, our legs flailing. Larry made a big show of squinting and yawning, as though he had slept through it all. And to be fair, it turned out to be only his own tail he had gnawed. Still, I don't think any of us believed he had done it unconsciously—and if he had, that was no less troubling: What might he do next?

"Where am I?" he asked. "What happened to my tail?"

Felicia spit at him.

"Look, Larry," I told him, "I think I speak for all of us when I say: This is unacceptable behavior."

"You've crossed the line, Larry," Felicia said. "You'd kill us if you could get away with it! Wouldn't you?"

Larry didn't answer, kept his face averted, licked his bloody fur.

Paul, not surprisingly, said nothing, but something made me turn and look at him. His eye appeared even larger than usual, and a dark light I'd never seen before seemed to tremble out of it, directly at me, a light that said, *Emergency—emergency*.

"Larry, I beseech you," I said. "For the good of your brethren—"

"Brethren, fuck," Felicia said. "He tried to kill us. If he tries it again I'll chew his face off."

Later that night when I finally got back to sleep, I dreamed of Paul's eye. Nothing else—no movement, no sound, just that black, unblinking orb, so large it filled my sea of vision, its fierce silence growing bigger, more palpable, more demanding every moment. Paul himself seemed absent; there was only the eye. *What*, I pleaded, *what do you want?,* but the eye gave no answer, nor did it ever turn its gaze away.

And in the morning, like some terrible omen, like a dark cloud, a rabid raccoon had appeared high over us, in the branches of our tree. It woke us up humming, crooning at some unnaturally low, thunderlike frequency. The smell of its disease was everywhere, heavy against our eyes, and the bugs were going nuts, leaping wildly out of the grass in all directions like gazelles.

"Is it raining?" Felicia asked. Water from the raccoon's mouth was falling on us, making marks on our backs.

"Listen!" Larry cried. "Listen to what it's saying!"

The end, the end, the end, the raccoon chanted. Its voice was unraveling, all-engulfing in its desperation; the words seemed to float down from something larger and more diffuse than the bloated, swaying shape on the branch.

"How much more of this are we supposed to take?" Felicia said. "I mean, is this why we were born—to be driven crazy by lunatics?"

The end, the end, sang the raccoon.

"We hear you, buddy!" Larry called up to it, but it did not appear to notice.

"Why were we even born?" Felicia repeated. "I need to

know. Can any of you answer me? Marv? Larry? Paul?" As she said each name, we all turned to look at that individual, and when she fell silent we were all left staring at Paul, as if he might really provide the answer. I can't speak for the others, but that's when I knew we were done for.

That was three days ago, and we haven't moved since. Our limbs are sore from gripping the tree, our necks stiff from looking up. The raccoon hangs over us, swollen with meaning, chanting out the end of its life. All the other creatures have fled the yard—only we five remain, locked in our fateful exchange. The raccoon chants and drools, Larry babbles, Felicia wails in frustration, and Paul's eye grows bigger and blacker, its message more inevitable, every moment. Larry was right: *The day of change is near.* I try to hold out hope that when it is upon us we will rise to meet it, and find it in ourselves to do whatever it is that's required of us.

II.

When he was a teenager he had longed to become a real doctor, and he still thought of it that way, despite his successful ten-year practice in the treatment of small animals: Real doctors treated human beings. It wasn't that he didn't care about animals, but it was humans he would truly have loved to save—the unsolvable enormity of them, the moist complexity and trickiness of even their simplest parts. One summer when he was still in high school he'd worked a minimum-wage custodial job at a convalescent home, cheerfully scrubbing bathrooms and changing linens and digging people's false teeth out of the cafeteria garbage. He loved helping others, and he was not undone by the grisly.

Then one day he was mopping the hallway outside the room of a retired actuary named Mrs. Rooney who had suffered a series of strokes that caused her to perceive a string hanging in her field of vision, whichever way she looked. She would constantly call the nurses and orderlies into her room to get the string out of her face, driving them crazy. On this day, she had soiled herself in her bed, and as he slopped his mop along the linoleum, he overheard her ask the nurse who was giving her a sponge bath to please be more gentle. "I'm not having a picnic down here," the nurse snapped.

He waited for Mrs. Rooney's response, heard nothing, waited a few seconds more, listening to the thick, ruined silence coming from that room, and then he left his mop standing upright in the bucket there in the hall. Looking back, if he had to pinpoint the exact moment he'd abandoned his plan, that would have been it. He could still see that mop standing there like a surprised person he had suddenly walked away from in the middle of a conversation.

He returned to the job, of course, worked the hours he'd signed up for and finished out his summer, but something in him, perhaps his will, had shifted, backed off, turned itself ever-so-slightly away from the experience. He had reported the nurse to the supervisor, but that didn't solve it for him. It wasn't the blood or shit or vomit, he eventually came to understand, that he couldn't handle—not the soft, vulnerable parts of people that undid him, but the hardness, for which there was no methodology, no cure.

So it was that now, instead of saving human lives, he specialized in rodents and birds, taught community education courses called "Understand Your Gerbil" and "What Your Finch Wants You to Know" and "Raising Orphaned Squirrel Babies So They Can Rejoin Their Brethren in the Wild." The only cases he found difficult were those brought about by ignorance: the old man who had shown up, for instance, with a starved, comatose baby squirrel he'd found in his driveway and tried to revive for two weeks; the thing refused to eat, the man said, sounding a little angry. The animal, just a few inches long, lay at the bottom of a large empty carton, a single, enormous unshelled walnut by its head.

Most of the cases the veterinarian saw struck him as a little silly, though of course he never let on that he felt that way in front of his anxious clients. Out of some perverse habit or compulsion, even after ten years, he often thought about the human equivalent of an operation he was performing or a treatment he was administering, forced himself to consider the differences between human and animal in terms of money, beauty, glory. When he heard about the squirrels that were being delivered for him to untangle, he recalled the story in the news about the surgical team who had, in a ten-hour operation, separated a set of human infants, conjoined twins who shared one six-chambered heart. The doctors had known in advance that only one of the babies could survive the surgery, they had selected which one based on all available information, and that baby's fingernails were painted pink to avoid a tragic mistake. Because of the sacrifice of life, the doctors were careful not to sound too celebratory in interviews. The head surgeon had said that the feeling he'd had during the procedure was "one of respect for the sanctity of the individual soul."

The veterinarian understood that he himself would never give such an interview, never know such a feeling—it was not a feeling likely to be engendered by inoculating a ferret, or, for that matter, untangling a bunch of squirrels from a grocery bag. Nevertheless, he tried to do his best by his small patients; someone had to do it. Cases came to him, unglamorously, and he took them.

The tangled squirrels had turned up in a humane cage trap someone had set for a rabid raccoon, a guy from the newspaper had gone out to take a photo, and then Don Harbison from Animal Control had picked them up and brought them in for the surgery. "I'd say these little 'brethren' are *unblessed*," Harbison said, holding the wire cage up over the receptionist's desk and peering in at the jumbled gray lump of bodies. The Animal Control guys were a hardcore crew, and Harbison in particular liked to rib the veterinarian about the hokeyness of his community-ed courses. The squirrels didn't flinch at Harbison's loud laughter; they looked wary and exhausted.

But the operation turned out to be a simple one, no complications—it wasn't even a surgery, really, so much as a clean-up job, the cutting away of a lot of hair and debris, the sterilization of a superficial bite wound on one of the tails, rabies vaccines for all. The squirrels would be fine when the general anesthetic wore off, though their tails were somewhat diminished, bent at odd angles and half-bald. But here, the veterinarian felt, was one of the nice aspects of treating animals: Unlike humans, they would not feel shame about their deformities.

He thought about something he'd come across when he was putting together his "Orphaned Squirrel Babies" course, an old wives' tale that said the squirrel was the only animal in the Garden of Eden to witness Adam eating the apple. So horror-struck was this squirrel, the story went, that it pulled its naked, ratlike tail across its eyes to block out the sight, and as a reward, all squirrels were henceforth given bushy tails by God. The veterinarian idly wondered how the four he had just separated would manage to block out horrifying sights, but he couldn't imagine what those sights might be. Old wives' tales were really about people, anyway.

When the squirrels woke up, he carried them, in four separate rodent cages, out into the small, dogwood-shaded courtyard behind his office. He set the cages on the grass facing the line of trees along the back fence, opened and braced the cage doors, and then stood back to watch. After a long pause, all four squirrels scampered out at once, then moved in four different directions. Oddly, though, they seemed to move in perfect unison. They took miniature roller-coaster-shaped hops, then stopped to stand on their hind legs, then bounded forward again, all at the same moments, as if mechanized. They didn't seem to be aware of one another, didn't even glance at one another, which for some reason made the veterinarian smile.

The biggest of the four was the first to break formation, disappearing in a sudden burst over the fence and into the forest preserve. Two others followed more cautiously, going off at divergent angles into the brush. The last, who the veterinarian noticed had unusually large eyes, lingered a few seconds longer, standing up motionless with his paws against his breast and gazing off into the distance as though he were listening to something the others had not heard. Then he, too, made his careful way into the sheltering foliage, looking back once at the veterinarian, or perhaps at the building or the row of empty cages.

Respect for the sanctity of the individual soul, the veterinarian thought. What a joke.

Still, he felt decent. To have done his part, however small anyone might judge it. On his drive home he sang nonsensically along with radio songs he didn't know, then detoured on impulse to the apartment of a woman he had dated briefly, months ago. He had never understood why the relationship trailed off. She was a sharp-eyed girl who had worked as his assistant for a summer and then taken a much better job at the children's zoo across town. They'd quarreled a lot while they were dating, yet there had been something genuine between them from the start, some sort of recognition, though of what the veterinarian could not have said. Often, she said something he had just been thinking, or they both spoke the same words at once. He still suffered occasional bouts of missing her, fits of melancholic happiness or happy melancholy that seemed to come out of nowhere, like this one, and as he stood on her front step in the late-day sun, waiting to see if she was home, he wondered again, as he often had in the past, whether in some nameless but essential way they were meant to be together.

ARE WE ALMOST THERE

I MET YOU first when I was six and you were in utero. You weren't there yet. I was six and a half and in Florida on my first vacation by plane. In O'Hare Airport my mother gave me a spoonful of bitter yellow Dramamine and then held me up to the drinking fountain, and the icy metallic water got the bad taste out of my mouth. The medicine made me drowsy but still I was scared. How will the plane stay in the air, I asked. How will they understand us in Florida—do they speak another language there. My father talked to me in his peaceful way about engineering. He spoke as though he personally knew lots of engineers and liked and admired all of them. Engineers were great men, he seemed to be say-ing. My mother, who tended to scorn things, laughed at my other question. Of course they speak English, it's not an-other *country,* she said—everyone knows that. Their an-swers were pleasant, relieving, like that mouthful of cold water after the Dramamine, but fleeting. Everything was fleeting.

We took two planes. The first plane was big, like being in a house. It was not really moving, apparently. I sat between my mother and father in a row of three orange seats and was given a strange pillow that seemed to be made out of paper. We got blue rubber headphones that felt like Gumby and we listened to Bill Cosby. It was odd. Bill Cosby was not talking out loud into the air, but separately to each one of us, only he was saying the same things. We weren't hear-ing him together and yet we were. We laughed into each other's faces at the same moments.

After that plane we took a very small plane that roared beneath us and seemed to be going terribly fast, just faster and faster, over water. I felt that I was trying to hold on to something, though I couldn't say what. It was getting harder and harder to hold on, the faster and faster we went. *We're almost there, we're almost there,* the grown-ups kept telling me, not only my parents but other adults on the plane, their kind faces leaning in as we went faster and faster, *We're almost there, we're almost there,* and I tried to hold on but finally couldn't anymore and as we rushed in and down to the runway I threw up into a white bag some- one held for me. Then I was given more water and every- thing went back to normal.

The motel overlooked a beach of seashells, and at the end of the shells was the water. No sand could be seen on the beach, only shells. This was rare, it was explained to me, something to be appreciated. Not too many people knew about this place, but we knew about it. Behind the motel was an endless hilly park with winding paths and regularly spaced white cinder-block structures that looked like iden- tical, fierce little houses but which actually contained only pipes, my father explained; I was happy to hear that, because I wouldn't have wanted to live in one of those little houses. In the evenings, right after dinner, sprays of water appeared everywhere, crisscrossing and arching over one another, some tall and fine and waving like the tails of exotic birds, and some shooting relentlessly in one direction, feeding the green dips and rises. From our room's patio I looked, but it hurt a little—my eyes, or chest or something. The color was so deep, so wet, the hills like mounds of wet green cake. I felt you out there somewhere, amidst all that green, but I couldn't see you, no matter how I concentrated. If I looked away, something would move in the corner of my eye, but when I looked back, you were never there.

But when I turned around to go back into the room there was a decal of a diving woman on the sliding glass door, right there at my eye level, strangely, as though someone had known I would be there to see it, and it let me know the door was closed and I had better open it or I would bump my head. The woman wore a pink bathing suit exactly like my mother's and the ugly white kind of bathing cap that strapped under her chin and covered practically her whole head. She was a little faded, peeling, like she had been stuck on there for years, though she did not appear to be an old woman. Her back arched gracefully and her toes were pointed, still, after all this time.

After breakfast our first morning I couldn't wait to get to the beach; I must have believed you would be there, for I'd heard the way people talked about it all the time, *the ocean, the ocean,* as though it were the point of everything. But two men were playing Jarts in the gravel parking lot of the Pancake Shack, which we had to cross to reach the path down to the water. *Be careful, those are young men,* my father said, as though that alone made the men suspicious, but they didn't look young to me—they were big men with long hair, far away and barely moving, and I had to get to you. *Watch it, don't run across there,* my mother said, jerking her arm out, but some kind of dark light shot through me and I got under it and ran. For a moment everything whirled whitely around me—I won!—but then something hit my head, hard, knocked me down.

Then the grown-ups were around me again, saying *Stop screaming, stop screaming,* and my hands were pried away from my eyes, and the first thing I saw was my mother comforting the young men, who appeared devastated. *I'm sorry, I'm sorry,* they kept saying, kicking at the ground as though they were angry at the rocks and pebbles. What were they so upset about? I wondered. They didn't even know me. My father had me by the shoulder, his face larger and closer than I'd ever seen it before as he poked at the place between my eyes with the tip of his index finger. *It hurts!* I cried. *Then stand still for once!* he snapped. *She's lucky she's not blind,* everyone was saying. *Close call,* they said. We returned to our room without speaking, as though we had been watching a play and now the play was over.

That afternoon we went not to the beach but to the motel pool, where they could watch me. I wore a butterfly-
closure Band-Aid over the bridge of my nose, importantly,
though I was disappointed that the closure in no way resembled a butterfly. Some other children were playing in the
shallow end, fighting over an inflated purple sea monster,
but they were of no concern to me—some of them were fat
and looked like they smelled, even in the clean blue water,
and the sea monster didn't look real. It was *smiling*. So I
took my raft to the deep end and played alone, whispering
to myself as usual, and when the wave or whatever it was
came up, I went under silently. One moment I was on top,
the canvas firm and bouncy beneath me, the world around
me hot and dry and sparkly with noise and light, and the
next moment the ropes were sliding through my fingers,
leaving me, everything fleeting again, and I grabbed but
there was nothing to grab, no raft, no ropes, only the warm
shapeless air—you weren't there yet. Then I hit the wall of
cold and everything went blue, time and noise stopped, and
I knew to hold my breath, but something was getting inside
me, and this time I really couldn't hold on, couldn't hold on
another second.

The grown-ups got me out, tugged me up by my arms,

gasping, back into the world of sun and solid concrete. *She knew what to do, she knew exactly what to do,* they said. I was wrapped in a white terry-cloth robe and placed on a full-length lounge and given handfuls of Kleenex and a necklace of yellow candy beads, which I was suddenly too sleepy to care about. My whole body felt pleasantly heavy, my eyes were closing by themselves, and my palms and the soles of my feet tickled, as if something were leaking out through them. *She knew exactly what to do,* the grown-ups kept repeating, surrounding me in a circle with their lounge chairs, and they sounded oddly proud, as though I had passed an important test. I tried to stay awake to hear what else they would say, but the sun kept pressing me further down and away from their voices, the distant splashes and shouts and the scrapes of chairs playing faintly on in my ears, a reassuring sound track to a dream I was starting to have, perhaps an early dream of you.

You couldn't have been far from me that day. I imagine you down near Cape Canaveral, still underwater yourself, the rushing of rocket engines echoing in your unformed ears, the anticipation of countdowns crackling invisibly all around you as you waited to be born. But yours is a peaceful generation, more patient and careful than mine, and you were probably just floating, hanging out, probably holding so still even then that your mother had begun to doubt her own senses, to wonder if she had imagined your very existence inside of her. And even if you did hear me go under, somehow, by radar or however babies know what they know before they're born, even if you made some heroic kick or twist to try to get to me, it's probably just as well that we didn't meet at that particular time. I was an only child, and babies gave me the creeps. They reminded me of mushy little aliens.

I MYSELF WAS an early baby, but not early enough. Four days earlier and I would have made it. As it was, I arrived in a bad year, a year of the Fire Horse. (I learned this decades later from a place mat at Happi Sushi.) I imagine myself trying to kick or dig my way out in time, get myself out of the fire, so to speak, and almost making it, but my mother, a no-nonsense woman with strong stomach muscles, was probably as usual doing everything she could to hold me back. But she couldn't have known about the Fire Horse. People born under the sign of the Fire Horse were basically doomed, the place mat said. *Illness, unhappiness, and bad luck follow these individuals and all those close to them,* it said. *Women in Asia born under this sign used to find it simply impossible to find mates.* (I've taken great strength from that "used to"—stored it away and carried it around like a roll of Life Savers in my brain.) At any rate, once I was born there was no turning back—only forward to go, always forward, and with only the ghost of a promise that you or some version of you might eventually catch up with me.

But you were running behind right from the start, a late baby, I'll bet, refusing to budge or show your face for weeks past your due date and driving your poor mother nearly insane. So it's no surprise that the second time we met we were still out of sync; really, it's a miracle we met at all. I was on vacation again, always on vacation when I ran into you, always somewhere hot and tropical, never in the cold dirty city back home.

Actually, now that I think about it, there was a boy I met once for five seconds at a Chicago Old Town School of Folk Music Winter Singalong that might have been you. I hated those events: crowded, steamy, smelly affairs where we were given the sheet music to songs no one ever heard of about children in other countries doing humorless, inexplicable things. And what was the point of singing if we had to read the words as we went? All I cared about was the juice and cookies afterward, but I was allowed only two when I could easily have eaten many more—I was like the Cookie Monster when I was supposed to be more like Grover, but Grover got on my nerves.

I was wearing a new necklace I had begged for, an extremely realistic-looking plastic squirrel that fit perfectly in the palm of my hand, strung on a genuine rawhide cord. The squirrel was clutching an acorn the size of his head, but he wasn't eating the acorn, just holding it against his white chest. His enormous brown-black eyes were wide open and he had just a tiny smile, as though he were very satisfied. I was stuck in the damp noisy crush of grown-ups and children trying to get close to the cookie table, but I was occupying myself with my squirrel, when I sensed someone watching, breath against my skin. A little brown-haired boy was standing right next to me, nearly on the toes of my sneakers. He was staring at my squirrel, and he looked like he was about to cry. His eyes were as big as the squirrel's, but darker, much darker, just impossibly dark. I gasped and grabbed automatically at my chest, but my hand hit the squirrel instead. And then it was as if I had no choice. I had to give it to him. It was going to kill me to give it to him, but

I had to give it to him. I pulled it off fast, as I would with a Band-Aid so it wouldn't hurt as much or for as long, and pushed it into his hands. He looked startled, even terrified, but his hands were holding on to it tightly and he didn't say anything, and then my mother was suddenly there and I was led away. She did not seem to have seen the boy, and she never asked about the squirrel—I wondered later if I had imagined the whole episode. I'm still not sure. But maybe that wasn't even you.

I'm positive about the other time, though, the tropical vacation. It was Easter and I was with my parents in Cancún, Mexico, before people knew about it; we were always going places that were going to be big someday but only we knew about them. The island was just a strip then, hotels and discos on one side, wild land and water reservoir on the other where my parents could go look at birds through binoculars. I was twelve and found that hobby boring, pathetic, embarrassing, and pitiable. Nature had become slightly disgusting, unnatural. Our room at the El Presidente filled with appalling bugs each night, some the size of small animals. I did not think it unreasonable to scream at the sight of these, but the third or fourth time I did it my father actually began shaking me, gripping my shoulders and yelling, "Do you need a *psychiatrist!*" He let go after a moment, not seeming to expect an answer, and I sank into rattled silence. No one had ever talked about psychiatrists before. I did not want a psychiatrist. I wanted a tan, a true, sinister tan and all that went with it, all they could not begin to comprehend, all that would bring me closer to you.

Don't overdo it on the first day, my mother warned, but I ignored her and took my raft—not the same raft I'd had in Florida but a silvery rubber reflector one designed to tan my hidden crevices without me having to expose them—out into the Caribbean. The day was brilliant, the sun larger and hotter than it had been in Florida or ever was up north, the waves small and salty and easy to negotiate, and the further out I got the shinier and more beautiful everything became. Nothing was required of me, nothing scrutinized. I slept out there for hours, dreaming of nothing at all.

When I came in that evening I was full of forgiveness: my father, mother, even the bugs, were no longer a problem. I was finally, thoroughly warm. My eyes were warm. My body was perfect. I was a gift, a free-floating charm, gold and silver and ready to go. I floated through dinner at the hotel restaurant, smiling at the Spanish-speaking waiters and busboys, who smiled back as though we shared a secret, and I smiled at my shiny face and hair in our bathroom mirror over a sink full of beautiful glittery slow-moving gnats, and I fell into sleep between starched white sheets, still smiling.

I dreamed that a train was trying to run over my finger, and I woke up vomiting. *She overdid it,* my mother said, somewhere behind me, and I let loose again and was wiped with clean towels and wrapped in clean sheets and when I woke up later the first thing I saw was a small green bottle of Wink soda, which I had never heard of but which I drank and which was so alarmingly good that tears came to my eyes. I was freezing cold and dying of thirst. "You overdid it," my mother said from the doorway. "We're going bird-watching, see you later."

I ate a salty ham sandwich that had been left on a paper plate beside the Wink and decided to be gone when my parents returned. I was shaky getting into my clothes, but I looked great. My face gave off an unearthly pink glow, making my eyes appear greener in contrast, and my legs, coming out of white cutoffs, while not as brown as I'd hoped, seemed animated from within. They moved friskily against one another in the elevator as though of their own accord.

The lobby shocked me. The elevator doors opened and it was as though I'd been sleepwalking and was now shaken awake, mid-stride. Pillars I hadn't noticed before rose up whitely around me, larger than any pillars I'd ever seen, leading up to the stucco ceiling a hundred miles away. Tinted glass walls let in the blue glare of ocean and sky and the painful silvery flash of cars parked in the lot. But I'd been through here a dozen times already, so why were my ears ringing, my stomach dropping? *The elevator,* I thought desperately, *the sunstroke,* but neither was it. Mexican people moved around me at a regular pace, wearing pants and shirts and speaking Spanish to one another in ordinary tones, as though nothing unusual were happening. No one glanced at me, which made the sensation worse.

I remembered a dream I'd had the year before. I'd been in the white-and-glass lobby of a hotel, this lobby or one exactly like it, my mother and father somewhere in the background, and it had been a bright still day just like this one, with crowds of people milling around, guests of the hotel and workers carrying stacks of clean white towels, and then word came that the nuclear bomb had been dropped. The news did not come over a radio or by anyone announcing it, it just came, as things do in dreams, and although the day was continuing brightly and evenly on without smoke or noise, the people began quietly dying all around me, guests and workers alike lying down on the carpeted platforms near the check-in desk or sinking into the bland lobby armchairs, giving in to the invisible radiation or poison that was everywhere. Nobody screamed or reached out to one another, they just lay down, one by one, everywhere I looked, and just as it occurred to me that I was still alive, my stomach began to ache, and I knew that meant the end. I got down on the floor on my back and closed my eyes, hoping the end would come quickly or miss me altogether, thinking I was already dead, but there was no tricking the end, no getting around it. It was not a person or even in any way personal. A siren of two alternating tones came on in my head, my hands and feet began to tingle and burn, and I felt myself shrunken and translucent, moving upward through my body, then coming up like a sweater over my own head. Then there was just darkness, and the siren over and over for what seemed like forever.

It had taken me weeks to recover from that dream, my stomach clenching and my hands and feet burning whenever I heard a police siren, and now it was finally upon me. My head filled with an awful rushing pressure, some enormous wave rising and breaking before my eyes, but then, just as I surrendered to it, a voice off to my left said, "Hey."

I blinked and opened my eyes and there you were.

A skinny brown-haired boy about my size was sitting in one of the armchairs. He was very dark—might have been Mexican but his eyes were blue—and he was staring directly at me. But unlike the boy at the singalong, this boy didn't appear needy. He appeared unalarmed, expectant. He was just looking at me, expecting me to say something.

"You know that song 'Tide Is High,'" I said.

"Yeah," he said. His voice was deep, like a teenager's, though he looked no older than me.

"I *love* that song," I said and immediately felt my face burn, though he did not seem taken aback. "I mean I like it, it's cool," I said quickly.

"Yeah," he said. He turned and gazed out the window at a family with several children getting out of a station wagon, but he didn't seem to be in any hurry to leave. His skinny arms rested on the fat arms of the chair.

"Is that your family?" I asked. "Do you have to go?"

He shook his head. "I'm here with my high school. We have chaperones but they don't care what we do. They let us party in their room. We went to a disco and they were dancing on the tables."

"Chaperones?" I said. "What is that, is that Spanish?"

"No, they're just teachers," he said. "From my school. But it's not illegal or anything, there's no drinking age here, you know? So they can't get in trouble. It's cool, I guess." He looked tired, suddenly, almost sad. "You take one of those motorbikes yet?"

"Motorbikes, no," I said.

"We can rent one," he said and seemed to perk up a bit. He sat up in the armchair and leaned forward, wringing his hands together between his knees, his eyes fixed on mine. "It only costs a dollar for the whole day and you can ride to the end of the island."

"We're allowed to just go and rent one?" I said. "How long does it take to get to the end of the island? This is like a *motorcycle*?"

"No, motor*bike*," he said. "It's smaller than a motor-cycle. It's fun. Let's go, come on." He jumped up and stood there, waiting, apparently only for me.

"They just let kids rent them?" I said. I wanted him to give me a sign, though I could not have said what kind.

"Yeah, it's safe and everything," he said. "I'm fourteen," he added.

"Really?" I said. It was amazing. Fourteen was so old, but he didn't look old at all. It was as if he had just been sitting there waiting, perhaps refusing to move or get any bigger until I got there, but how could he have known me, or known that I would arrive at that moment? I wanted to ask, but he had turned and was already heading for the sliding glass doors.

I hurried up behind him. Already I couldn't picture his face. "Where are you *from*?" I asked.

"New Jersey," he said. "My name's Jamie."

"New Jersey," I repeated tonelessly. I didn't know anyone from New Jersey, New Jersey meant nothing to me, I got no mental picture whatsoever. I felt fine, though, oddly. The day held still all around us, silent and almost unbearably bright as we stepped out into it.

But the ride was loud and fleeting; we could not speak over the motor and I had to concentrate on too many things at once. Jamie seemed happy steering us along, his hair blowing back against my cheek, but I was kept busy hanging on to his wiry torso and holding my feet up and figuring out where to position my head. Scenery whipped greenly, gloriously by around us, but I was missing most of it. At one point something large and white tumbled suddenly into our path and I shut my eyes, waiting for the crash, but there was just a hollow thumping sound and we kept going. "What was that?" I screamed. "Lampshade!" Jamie yelled, in his deep voice. Then he said something else, but I couldn't hear him.

"What did you say?" I shouted. "It made you nervous?"

"No, I said *I ran over it on purpose*!" he yelled.

When we got to the tip of the island we just turned around, unceremoniously, and started back. On our turn-around, the wooden heel of my platform sandal knicked the ground and a piece flew off, my fault for not lifting my foot in time.

"Some of the other kids are going swimming tonight," Jamie said, back at the El Presidente. We were idling in the parking lot. I got off the bike, my legs vibrating.

"You're inviting me," I said. "When."

"Later," he said vaguely, looking off at something across the road. His eyelashes were the longest I'd ever seen on a boy, black and perfectly straight, and I suddenly remembered the squirrel boy but thought, *No, couldn't be, his eyes were brown.* I looked where he was looking, following an imaginary line in the air that started with his eyelashes, but I didn't see anything out there in the brush. When I looked back at him, he had already turned around and was pushing off with his foot, wobbling a little as he pulled away.

Everything I touched back in our room—the light switch, dresser handles, even a glass—gave me a small, audible shock, though the room was too humid for static. The vibrating in my legs had not stopped. I tried to imagine his face again, but already it was fading, and the more I tried, the more elusive it became, like trying to picture infinity. Yet I sensed more strongly than ever that we were almost there, I only had to wait a little longer. I put on my bikini and sat on the edge of the bed, shivering with sunburn. There were only a few more hours to go. The room hummed; I was ready.

"Are you ready to go to Chichén Itzá?" my mother asked. We were at dinner; I'd had to get dressed again. She took a large bite of molé chicken, her cheek bulging out as she chewed it. I watched the bulge, disgusted, uncomprehending. *Chichén Itzá*. What was she saying, was she speaking another language? Then I remembered. We were going to see the Mayan ruins—important rocks. We were leaving that evening, renting a car.

"I don't want to go," I said.

"You have no choice," my father said. He had already finished and was pushed back a few inches from the table, his eyes half-closed, his napkin wadded on his empty plate.

I've often wondered if what I did at the ruins was in some way responsible for how things turned out between you and me, but there doesn't seem to be any logical, scientific way of proving it. I stole a rock. Not a regular rock from the ground, but a reddish, gumball-sized fragment of the ruins themselves. I picked it up for no reason and put it in my jean-jacket pocket, where it rode, forgotten, back home with me, and I saved it for years, though it was not impressive or even significant-looking. Still, taking it had definitely been against the rules. Signs had been posted everywhere, in Spanish and English, but I had paid no attention to the signs. The ruins were so enormous, after all, unfathomably large, and the red stones and pebbles covered everything as far as a person could walk or see, like snow. And the piece I took was so tiny, I could not see how it could be considered stealing. What were they worried about, anyway, I wondered—whoever "they" were. That eventually, stone by stone, the entire Mayan ruins would be taken away? That was simply not rational.

Nevertheless, I didn't mention what I'd done to anyone until college, when, drunk one night, I confessed to a guy I knew who majored in anthropology and kept his deceased border collie's skull, which he'd boiled and cleaned himself, in his truck's glove compartment—he seemed like someone who might not be bothered by certain things. "That's it?" he said, when I told him. "Everyone does that."

"Really?" I said. I felt suddenly and inexplicably relieved.

"Absolutely," he said. "Every single person I know who's been there has done that." He stared at me then, considering. "You are the only person I know who took it so seriously, though," he said.

Either way, cursed or not, when we returned to Cancún, Jamie was gone. We'd only been away three days, but it seemed like centuries. I looked for him everywhere—by the pool, in the lobby, up and down corridors on every floor, my heart pounding and my hands sweating so badly I had to keep going back to the room and washing them, but there was no evidence of him anywhere. Nothing even looked familiar. After a while, I wasn't sure whether it would be more of a relief to see him or not to see him. I couldn't imagine how I would act if I finally found him, what I would say. The motorbike ride now seemed a brief, hazy dream. I was working myself up into a tizzy, my mother would have said. Yet I couldn't believe it was over so quickly, that he hadn't left some sign.

Finally, I remembered the high school, the chaperones— they *had* to be real. But the clerk at the front desk was Mexican; how could I communicate with him? I prepared to use a kind of sign language: I would hold my hair up and away from my face so I resembled a *boy,* Jamie.

The man was writing something in Spanish in a ledger as I stepped up. I spoke loudly, clearly, and slowly. "I'm trying to find someone I know," I said.

"Yes, can I help you?" he said, snapping his head up. He spoke perfect English; it was my own voice that sounded broken, unfamiliar. It was hard to get the words out.

"Those kids from New Jersey . . ." I said.

"They left," he said. He scratched his head and glanced around as though he expected to see them floating past in the air. I waited, not breathing. "They were good kids," he said finally. He smiled quickly, almost wistfully, and looked back down at his ledger, nodding after a moment as though confirming something. I backed away and fell into the armchair, lining my arms up evenly on the chair's arms as Jamie had done. I looked out the window, trying again to see whatever it was he saw, but there was nothing to see, only the green land around the reservoir across the street, and the blue sky over that, stretching endlessly away behind the water. I thought of the last thing he'd said to me: *Later. When?* I thought, but no answer was forthcoming.

AFTER THAT I was in high school and took no more tropical vacations with my parents—I fought to be allowed to stay home, the fights sometimes ending with my mother and me literally chasing each other around the house. She was beginning to drive me crazy. "We're going to the Kakamega Forest, don't you want to go to the Kakamega Forest?" she would scream, and I would think *The rip-your-face-off forest* and slam my bedroom door in the nick of time as she rushed up the stairs behind me. As if to placate both of us, the Chicago winters grew preternaturally warm, apparently a result of El Niño, which I had never heard of. The TV newscasters loved it. "Birds don't know which way to fly, flowers are fooled into blooming," they announced. "Blame it on 'The Child'!" I took melancholy walks in December through melting snow under a sun that seemed weary, but I never ran into you. I had begun having a recurring nightmare in which I could not turn off the clock radio by my bed. The knob would come off in my hand, and then I'd pull the plug out and hurl the radio onto the floor, but the cord would rise up like a cobra and wave menacingly in my face. The radio would be playing some stupid song, something by Elton John, or "Listen to the Music" by the Doobie Brothers, a song that was not in itself scary, though it was scary that I couldn't make it stop.

By college I had given up on you altogether and occupied myself with substitutes—poor substitutes, and I'm sorry for what I did with some of them, but everyone was as lost as I, it seemed. "You know, you have a kind of sly dignity," a guy I dated once commented. "You know what I like about you?" another said. "You walk loudly and carry no stick whatsoever." I liked that guy, actually, but he didn't want to date me, it turned out; he was just amusing himself before going off on an Alaskan fishing boat with his real girlfriend, a basketball player named Hikmet, which was Turkish for "All things come from God." It seemed hopeless.

"When is someone going to take care of me?" I asked the dog-skull guy one night, but all he said was, "Maybe you should *let* them."

"That's the dumbest thing I ever heard," I told him. "Would you tell the starving children in Africa to *let* someone feed them?"

"Well, maybe someone *is* taking care of you," he said.

"What does that mean?" I said. But he just shrugged, and would say no more. He had his skull, all he seemed to need.

I even tried an Eagle Scout, thinking those regimented types might be onto something, after all: service, steadfastness, and mundane but integral survival tricks—starting fires, tying knots, recognizing important constellations. "You know, 'Smoke on the Water' is my favorite song to get a blow job to," the Eagle Scout told me, as though he were sharing a wildly exciting secret. And even he was a good soul, always patting me nicely on the head before I left to go back to my dorm; certainly he meant me no harm. We were all muddling through, doing the best we could, supposedly.

I comforted myself with the words to that old song: *If you can't be with the one you love, honey . . .*

But now it seems to be getting later and later, the memory of you more and more distant, and I'm finding it hard to recall what you even look like, if I ever knew. Sometimes when I'm in some waiting room, at the doctor's or the Department of Motor Vehicles, I'll think I see you suddenly out of the corner of my eye—the toe of someone's loafer or the cuff of their pants, an arm or leg flashing by in the doorway—and I jump up, knocking ashtrays and magazines to the floor, making people stare. But it's never you, and sometimes no one is there at all.

Where are you, and why haven't you given me some sign? I imagine you still a child, a boy sleeping somewhere on pale sand, desert or beach, camped out in a faded sleeping bag beneath your favorite star (it kills me that I don't even know which one it is), unaware that you're late for someone else's life, or even that someone else is waiting, always waiting, still waiting for you after all these years. But nothing will wake you, no nightmares trouble that kind of sleep, the honest sleep of children or those in time with their own lives.

Last night, I dreamed you ran over me with your

skateboard. I heard you coming up the street but I couldn't move, I was just lying there on the sidewalk under the orange tree outside my apartment, the gravelly roar of your wheels growing louder and louder in my ears, the night sky black and still and starry between the branches of the tree, and though I kept trying, I couldn't turn my head to see you finally coming, to let you know I knew, so I just tilted it back as far as I could, exposing my throat, and shut my eyes, waiting for your wheels to hit my jugular vein. *I surrender,* I thought, but I was not scared, only weak and exhilarated, your grinding, crescendo roar rattling my whole body—and then I woke up, and you still weren't there.

I couldn't bear to open my eyes, so I thought of something totally unrelated, a mental trick I've learned. I thought of a movie I hadn't seen in years, *Snoopy, Come Home,* the one where Snoopy runs away from home and stays with a sick girl in the hospital, cheering her up. She was his original owner, or maybe she just thinks she was, I don't remember exactly. Maybe she just wants to adopt him. She may be the same person as the little red-haired girl, or a character later known as Lila—it's unclear. Anyway, the whole time Charlie Brown is going out of his mind looking for Snoopy, Snoopy and this girl are sitting around on her hospital bed feeling sorry for each other, eating candy and listening to sad music. The girl is pretty, of course, and very nice to Snoopy, but she's slightly annoying. She has no sense of humor, she's just kind of sugary sweet. In the end, Snoopy makes the right decision and goes home with Charlie Brown. The girl only wanted him for consolation, the movie implies, because she was so weak. Still, she behaves well when Charlie Brown comes to pick Snoopy up, and all three of them are weeping by the time they say their good-byes. When I saw this as a child, I remember, I wept also, but I couldn't seem to get up and turn off the TV, my body was stuck.

And last night, lying in bed with you not there yet, I began to cry like that again, only angrier. *Snoopy, Come Home,* I thought. Who had come up with such a concept, and what in the world were they thinking? At least an hour and a half, which would seem like years to a child, of Charlie Brown waiting for that dog, trying to find him, giving up, trying harder, giving up again, nearly going insane. *If I don't find that dog soon,* he kept saying, *I'll go crazy!*

We were just children, you and I, just little kids in the seventies, sitting around in our flannel pajamas, eating our bowls of Honeycombs or Lucky Charms, digging through the box for the hidden prize—just kids. *The people who made that movie,* I thought. *My God, what were they trying to do? Kill us?*

The Cantankerous Judge

It was my dream to someday go before the Cantankerous Judge. Everyone who went before him, even those he humiliated, loved the Cantankerous Judge, and appeared changed by him. He was older, balder, and less photogenic than the other TV judges, and of no identifiable ethnic or regional origin: the larynx-amplifying box he relied on made his voice seem to come from everywhere and nowhere at once, like the unsettling sound produced by one of those Tibetan monks who could sing two notes simultaneously. His decisions were incomprehensible, merciless, and nearly impossible to predict, yet as they were delivered one could see on the shiny, shifty-eyed, overly made-up faces of the litigants, even on the pushed-in faces of the doomed, expensive little dogs and cats they sometimes held, a breaking wave of essential truth, a kind of rearrangement of self being enacted in their features, perhaps even at the level of their molecules. The Cantankerous Judge kicked other TV judges' butts—both figuratively, in the ratings, and literally: he was frequently cited in the tabloids for provoking one or another of his competitors to fisticuffs at some L.A. hot spot, even the Lady Judge, though this behavior went against everything she advocated in her best-selling book, *Talking Yes, Hitting No.* The Cantankerous Judge didn't have a book. "It is not necessary for me to write one," he said simply and enigmatically in interviews.

The Cantankerous Judge could deliver a folksy, admonishing one-liner as effectively as his TV rivals the Ex-Hillbilly Judge and the Angry Black Judge, even in that odd, automated voice—for example, I once heard him tell the members of a litigious family that they were "*all* crazy, from Daddy on down!"—but this was not his métier. His specialty was sudden, relentless, highly personalized excoriation, followed by the even more sudden, seemingly careless bestowal of dizzying, impersonal forgiveness. This was just my interpretation, of course. But it was evident from watching his program, which was shown in syndication on UHF several times a day, that his popularity was fueled by the mistaken but stubbornly persistent belief that he couldn't *really* be that cantankerous, couldn't really be *that* cantankerous. What people loved about cantankerousness, after all, was how it reassuringly implied its opposite, the hidden heart of gold, the warm fuzzy center. People entered the Cantankerous Judge's courtroom knowingly, winkingly, but whereas they left the other TV judges' courtrooms predictably sullen or triumphant, here they came away, winners and losers alike, with the stripped look of tornado survivors, like they'd had the wind knocked out of them, or perhaps knocked *into* them—the terrifying wind of truth and change. At least, that was my interpretation.

And, in my view, they deserved it. These people, the defendants and plaintiffs, were hopelessly, pathetically, unironically attached to their material possessions. They were herd-mentality consumers, the kind of people my Pop Culture professors warned us about, the people I was referring to in my dissertation as "the masses." Their cases, viewed collectively, made up an encyclopedia of the trivial: *Divorce forced them to sell their tropical-pet collection— but now the reunited lovebirds want their lovebirds back.*

She says she paid for delivery, so she doesn't want to have to go to China to get her China hutch. His landlord was a co-median, but no one was laughing when the phone bill came. I had no sympathy for these people, whose pathological ac-quisitiveness had earned them the opportunity to meet the Cantankerous Judge, while my moral superiority and intel-lectual privilege meant I would never get that chance.

In my fantasy, I stood alone before the bench as neither defendant nor plaintiff, but as acolyte. The Cantankerous Judge's enormous Oz-like face floated over me in a bath of white-hot TV light, gazing down at me, *through* me, for long moments. Then, that half-human, half-mechanical voice would deliver its judgment, the impact of which would cause me to swoon. I couldn't imagine what he might say, but whatever it was would solve everything, absolve me of any petty vanities or slippery little sins that had managed to sneak under the radar of my rational, agnostic morality, such as the practice of hurrying to get in the grocery check-out line before someone else, or the belief that I actually deserved whatever nice thing had happened to me that day.

This was kid stuff, I knew, the kind of minutiae Catholic five-year-olds and scrubbed-face What-Would-Jesus-Do teenagers worried about, but on the other hand, as I was pointing out in my dissertation, one only had to look to popular music to locate more counterintuitive, aesthetically sophisticated expressions of this belief system, such as Stevie Wonder's 1976 hit "I Wish," a subtly deceptive paean to all the times Wonder did something wrong as a kid and got caught. What was sweet was not the innocence of childhood, Stevie Wonder was subversively implying, but its guiltiness, not the freedom to transgress, but the joy of having something to transgress against, i.e., the moral certainty of grown-ups, as characterized by Stevie Wonder's mother, whose admonishments appear in every verse: *Boy, I thought I told you not to go outside!* It's the same thing he's getting at in "Signed, Sealed, Delivered I'm Yours" when he crows, not in sorrow but in ecstasy, *I've done a lot of foolish things! That I really didn't mean!*

This was what the Cantankerous Judge would restore to me—the burdensome, nauseating, ecstatic literal morality of childhood. I could see it on the shaken faces of his litigants as they left his courtroom, and I could feel myself moving further and further away from it each passing year of my life.

For Christmas my boyfriend Gary and I gave each other

T-shirts printed with the show's slogan: HERE COMES THE CANTANKEROUS JUDGE! We wore them ironically—we did everything ironically, we were grad students—but the Cantankerous Judge had truly played an important part in our courtship. "Most women don't like the Cantankerous Judge," Gary said admiringly on our second date, and I'd heard him brag the same to his buddies, whose girlfriends all thought the Cantankerous Judge was an asshole. We shared, I thought, an unspoken understanding that our devotion to the Judge, while by no means naïve or genuine, was on the other hand not entirely academic, not entirely ironic.

Lately, however, Gary seemed to resent my enjoyment of the Cantankerous Judge, plus everything else about me. We had lived together a year, but it was as if he had been sleeping all that time and had just now awoken to discover me, an annoying stranger making outrageous claims on his person. He stared at things he'd once loved about me, such as my hair and face, with a pained, perplexed expression; he winced at my grocery choices as I unpacked them from the bag. At least once a day, no matter what I was doing, he would creep up beside me and observe, his voice thick with disbelief and disdain, "You're doing that *now*?" He slammed cabinets. He quit showering, wiping his armpits with a washcloth at the sink instead because it was faster, he said. He slept for twenty hours, or didn't sleep at all. If I glanced at him, he screamed, "Nothing's wrong!"

I recalled reading in *People* about a famous model who was divorcing her famous athlete husband; she knew the marriage was over, she said, when she asked him one morning what he wanted to do for lunch and he answered, "It's very important for me not to have plans today." This couldn't be Gary's problem, though, as we never had plans, we were grad students. He drove a Chevy Service Center's courtesy van part-time and I lived off grants and fellowships. Our scruffy, tropical college town demanded almost nothing of us in the way of rent or ambition, though, so our poverty wasn't very stressful.

You may be cantankerous, but you're no Cantankerous Judge, I thought of saying, but the joke would have been wasted on him in his present mood. At least, I hoped it was a mood. I didn't like seeing him this way, not because it hurt my feelings, but because his seemed suddenly outsized, childish, embarrassing. He no longer reminded me of Johnny Fever, the DJ from *WKRP in Cincinnati,* with whom I had been deeply in love when I was twelve, positive I was singularly qualified to understand and satisfy him. Initially, Gary's resemblance to Johnny Fever had been what attracted me: the walrus mustache and grungy T-shirts, the sexy, world-weary bass voice, the total unflappability.

Now, suddenly, we couldn't even watch the Cantankerous Judge without getting into a fight. "What a hottie!" he would shout, whenever Bekki the Bailiff stepped into frame to hand the Judge some Polaroids or escort a disruptive litigant out of the courtroom, her heavy holsters jiggling against her khaki-trousered hips. He was obviously trying to make a point.

"Wedding ring," I said coolly, squinting at the screen. I wasn't trying to provoke him, only restore a vestige of our usual TV-watching posture of sneering and/or clinical distance.

"So?" Gary said. "It's part of her costume."

"Those are real guns, why wouldn't that be a real ring?"

"Like you've ever seen a real gun!" he yelled, and stormed out of our bedroom to go sleep on the futon.

The next night he woke me at three in the morning waving a machete in my face. He was sitting on me, his thighs scissoring my torso so I couldn't move, and when he saw I was awake he pulled the knife out of my face and began waving it in the air over his head, in a silent, strangely artificial, piratelike gesture. In the light coming in the window from the street I could see it was too long and wide to be one of our kitchen knives, but more resembled a prop, papier-mâché or cardboard wrapped in foil. But I could hear and feel the heavy, metallic swish it made cutting through the air. "Did I ever show you this?" Gary asked. His voice sounded higher than usual, like a shy but excited Boy Scout's—breathless, thrilled, and intimate. "My machete! It was under the mattress *the whole time!*"

It was my nature, like most people's natures, not to believe I was ever truly in danger. With the exception of elderly eccentrics—like the local lady who'd been in the news recently for having accidentally dropped an emergency note she'd carried in her purse for fifteen years that said "HELP, I'M KIDNAPPED" in Wal-Mart, triggering a statewide search—most people did not believe the worst could happen to them, even as it was in fact taking place. Now, I proceeded as if the situation were still essentially rational—it was impossible in the moment for my mind to make the leap to any other assessment. My chief emotion was annoyance. "Get off me," I said. I twisted my hips, knocking Gary off-balance, and he fell backward, holding the machete up and out of the way as though it were freshly painted.

"I'm just trying to *show* it to you," he said. "Jesus!"

"I don't want to see it now!" I said. I rolled out of bed with the sheet around me, like the actresses always did on soap operas. Soap-opera actors, I'd learned while researching my dissertation, had strings tied to their big toes during bedroom close-ups so the director could give them yank signals to start and stop kissing. "I'm going to sleep in the bathroom," I said.

"No, come on!" Gary cried, right behind me. "Give me a chance! I'll throw the machete away, okay? I'll throw it out the window!"

I slammed the bathroom door in his face, making a flimsy, hollow bang. He was going to stab the door, I was sure—some kind of half-assed gesture that would cost us our security deposit.

"*You* can throw it out the window!" he yelled. "Come on, come on out. You can throw the machete out the window, okay, so we can go back to bed. It's fine with me if you want to do that. Do you want to throw it out the window in there? Here, I'm giving it to you now so you can throw it out the window." The edge of the blade appeared under the door, slid forward against the white tile, then stopped. "Shit," Gary said. "The handle won't fit."

I opened the door. His face brightened and he jumped up from his crouch. "Here," he said, thrusting the knife at me. I leapt back—foolishly, I realized, since he was holding the blade, extending the handle to me. It was made of some dark, mottled metal, tarnished and unidentifiable, like something in a dream.

I shook my head. "I'm going to stay at a hotel."

He looked stunned. "What are you talking about?" he said. I brushed past him and he stumbled as though I'd really shoved him, his arms folding the knife up flat against his chest, his wrists crossing over it, martyrlike. "Obviously I'm the injured party," he said tearily. "*I'll* go to a hotel."

I recalled something a counselor had once told me: *The persecutor role often contains the "escape hatch" out of the "rescue triangle" dynamic.* "If you want to break up, just say so," I told Gary.

"That's not it," he wailed. "I was fired!" He slid theatrically down the wall, his sweaty back streaking the plaster. He smelled unfamiliarly of shoestring potatoes, I noticed— a greasy-sweet smell, like the inside of a lunchbox. "For cussing!" he added, from the floor.

He didn't use implied quotation marks around that word, as we usually did. Transplanted Northerners, we were always being scolded down here for "cussing." I said, "At the passengers?"

He looked offended. "No, that's the thing! I wasn't even talking to them, I was *talking* to the other drivers on the *road*. I want to know which one of those cell-phone-talking assholes reported me. Treating me like their fucking chauffeur. God help me—I mean *them*—if I find out." He stabbed the carpet beside him, making small ripping sounds. "Motherfuckers."

"Well, it's just a job," I said, "right?" I was glad to hear him cussing again but I wanted him to pull himself together.

But instead, before my eyes he seemed to shrink and melt, until he appeared literally, physically smaller than he had been moments ago. I witnessed this with dismay, then despair, because I recognized it from past romantic relationships, and it only ever meant one thing. "Please, sweetie," I begged. "You know how unattractive neediness is." It was true. We had joked about it, about the embarrassing face of Sally Struthers, the comic TV appeals of corrupt charities: *Yes, please send me a photo of a child the world has forgotten.* Romance, at least in my own heart and experience, flourished best when kept free of emotion, especially the more messy and grotesque ones.

But Gary had not gotten off the floor. He sobbed, "I want my mom!"

HE LEFT THE next day, caught a Greyhound to his mother's in St. Louis—a vacation, he said, but I figured we were through. She was one of those overly solicitous, sincere mothers, painful to talk to. "You sound like a very nice person," she always said to me on the phone, her excruciatingly polite tone somehow suggesting that the opposite was true. She made it sound like a challenge, like code.

When he was growing up, Gary had told me, he wasn't allowed fast food, but every so often if he complained too much his mother would announce brightly, "We're having McDonald's for dinner!"—only it always turned out to be homemade hamburger patties, soggy with bread crumbs, served on toasted white bread with carrot-stick "fries" on the side. Because of this, Gary said, he eventually quit bringing friends home to play. He also wasn't allowed toy guns and in desperation would sometimes eat around the edges of his peanut butter and jelly sandwich until it was a gun shape, with which he would shoot his brothers. These deprivations explained his love of pop culture, he said, and the focus of his dissertation, the spiritual and social significance of restaurant mascots.

So his fleeing to her now seemed like the ultimate act of surrender, an abandonment of his grown-up self and all it stood for, all I loved. Fine, I thought, one more breakup. I would do the things I always did after a breakup. I would read bad magazines all day, as though my unhappiness were a waiting room. I would avoid *WKRP,* then I would obsessively watch it. I'd tell my parents in New England, eventually, and they'd say, "Yes, we noticed you don't mention him anymore." I would throw myself into the final chapters of my dissertation, in which I was planning to posit Casey Kasem as a kind of anti–Johnny Fever, or anti–Cantankerous Judge: validating, cataloguing, and institutionalizing the consumerist masses' every idiotic whim. What felt saddest was not even the breakup itself so much as how the sadness of breakups had become so predictable.

A couple days after he left, I broke down and bought a copy of *Talking Yes, Hitting No,* which I had been avoiding out of loyalty to the Cantankerous Judge; I wanted to read the chapter about the man who was able to track down and murder his wife at a battered women's shelter because he re-

membered its secret location from when he had stayed there
as a child with his mother. "This was no accident," the Lady
Judge wrote in her analysis of the case, "it was an on-
purpose." The Cantankerous Judge would have offered
more profound commentary, though I couldn't imagine
what. Perhaps he would have been interested in the track-
ing-down aspect; he often compared people to animals, or
pointed out the animals they were. He used "child" as a
compliment and "animal" as an insult, though sometimes
he would abruptly switch and do the opposite.

A knock woke me from a nap on the couch, the Lady
Judge's book fallen open against my sternum, and I thought,
He'd better not think he can come back here. At the door,
though, were two strangers, both wearing blue hospital scrubs
with clipped-on IDs: a black woman holding a baseball bat,
and a dwarf drinking a can of Pepsi. "Sorry to bother you,
ma'am," the woman said. Her hair was styled into a tall cone
dotted with gold highlights, her brow an imposing, eaglelike
ledge. Her voice was surprisingly girlish. "We're waiting on
your husband," she said, "if you don't mind letting him know.
We been sitting out here for thirty minutes, and this gentleman
and myself have got to get to work."

"Wrong house," I began, but over the man's head, in my

driveway, I saw the familiar red stripe on the van, the perk-ily lettered COURTESY. It was idling, driverless, its windows down. "Where is he?" I said.

"Like I say, I hate to intrude," the woman said. "But we been out here this whole time he been in there."

The man crumpled his can. "Sorry," he said to me. "I know it's no food or beverage on board but I ain't on board and it is *hot*."

"You saw him come in here?" I said. I stepped out onto the walkway and they moved back politely. I peered back inside at my motionless rooms, my innocent furniture.

"He went around back," the woman said.

Together we tramped around the side of the house, sur-veyed the row of dried-up shrubs and weedy baby pines, the tiny patio slab. "He a drinker?" the woman said, behind me. I turned and eyed her baseball bat, blond wood that matched the glimmers in her hair, and she smiled shyly, held it out for me to admire like a piece of jewelry. She said, "My boyfriend gave me this for when I'm on late shift. Don't want nobody messing with me."

"He got that right," the man said. He pointed the smashed can at me. "You drive?" he asked. "Because if I'm not in Pathology by five-thirty, I'm toast."

"Was he acting drunk?" I asked the woman.

"I wouldn't say that," she said. "Just sweatin' real bad and jumpy, in a real big hurry. Ran in to the waiting area and yelled at us to *hustle*. Is he in the brotherhood? 'Cause he's got an aura like a Christian fellow, but he appeared to have his self extremely wound-up and in need of release. You all going through some changes, whatever whatever, but then let us use your telephone, all right."

"No, I'll take you," I said. "Both to the teaching hospital?" I wanted, suddenly, to get them out of there, away from whatever was going to happen. Not heroism, but damage control—or simple *courtesy*.

"Yes, ma'am," the woman said. "We the only ones. There was another lady talking to the mechanic but your husband didn't want to wait on her."

The man made a maître d' gesture at me and said, "After you, madam." I faltered a moment, thrown by the chivalry, and he said, "I know what you're thinking, you're thinking what's it like to be a dwarf."

"I wasn't thinking that," I said, but I hurried past his outstretched arm.

On the van's radio Stevie Wonder was singing "For Once in My Life," a good sign, I thought, climbing up into the

high driver's seat. The interior was corporate-smelling, vac-
uumed blue velour. Then, at the same instant that I saw it
was not the radio but the tape deck playing, the dwarf said,
"What do you know? He's back," and another voice, a
bottom-scraping, world-weary, love-strained voice that
seemed to come at me from everywhere and nowhere at
once, said my name.

"It's okay, stay where you are, you drive," Gary said,
hoisting himself up out of the back, from behind the last
row of seats. He was wearing his Cantankerous Judge shirt,
dark-stained at the armpits. I reached for my door handle
but he was already beside me, the machete dangling matter-
of-factly in his fingers. "I'm not in Kansas anymore," he
said cheerfully, "get it?" In the rearview, the two passengers
appeared unalarmed—and why should they be? She had
her bat, now resting on her lap; Gary had his machete. The
dwarf had put on a Red Sox cap and was chewing gum expectantly. *HELP, I'M KIDNAPPED*, I thought, but since I
had no note to leave, no trail of bread crumbs, I would have
had to communicate it to them telepathically. It was odd to
feel these thrills of fear, connected somehow to the presence
of strangers; it was as though, alone, Gary and I had been

living outside the world of normal emotions. "Well?" Gary said. "What are you waiting for?"

Also odd was how attractive he suddenly looked. His face had grown severe and manly again, stubbled like Johnny Fever's, and the way he had popped up out of the back reminded me of the first episode of *WKRP,* where Johnny makes his debut waking up on the floor behind a sofa. Maybe this wasn't a nervous breakdown, I thought desperately, maybe it was a marriage proposal, like on *America's Wackiest Marriage Proposals.*

"Come *on*," he shouted, "these people work for a living!" I put the van into gear, feeling precarious so high off the pavement; it might have been a tractor, or a Zamboni. "Yeah," Gary said, as if reading my mind, "how do you think I feel?"

The hospital was ten minutes away, a straight shot through the ugly commercial district on an overcrowded, rage-inducing four-lane lined by car dealerships, the Chevy Service Center included. I thought I saw police lights flashing there but was afraid to turn my head and look, at forty-five miles per hour with the knife shape glinting dully in my peripheral vision. I thought about bailing at a stoplight, but then what would become of the passengers? I felt suddenly and irrevocably responsible for them. The woman was telling Gary chattily about her first husband. "I'm fine now that he ain't there telling me what I ain't all the time," she said.

Gary nodded sympathetically, his body turned in his seat so he could watch both her and me. "Love can certainly hold you hostage," he said.

"You got that right," the dwarf agreed. "And if you beg for mercy you're just like a little gnat bothering God. Not even—you're like a gnat bothering *that* gnat."

It was rush hour and the sun was coming at us sideways, heating my face and lighting the busy hospital entrance so that it resembled the glowing portal of a spaceship, people streaming in and out. Ambulances and officials were everywhere, but no one had caught up with us or even looked at us funny. Our passengers were climbing down out of the sliding door, thanking us, moving safely, irretrievably, out of reach. It seemed important not to make a scene.

On the sidewalk, the woman leaned around Gary and called in through the window, "You take care of yourself, baby doll." She didn't meet my eyes but there was something unexpectedly tender and personal in her voice, and I felt tears start. I had noticed this phenomenon other times since I'd moved to the South, during other breakups and also right after my grandfather, who I loved, had died: black people, homeless people, and dogs would stop and stare at me on the street, give me special, significant looks, or speak to me with sudden kindness and intimacy, as if I were giving off a magic distress charge only they could see. Cats and white people were oblivious. And all Northerners.

Gary motioned with the knife for me to pull away from the curb. "Back to the Service Center?" I said, fake-casually, a last-ditch effort.

He just laughed. "Are you crazy?" he said. He pointed the machete west, toward the Panhandle, the road out of town. The tip of the blade ticked the windshield. "That way," he said, and I didn't dawdle. The van's engine rumbled up through the ball of my foot, as though I were the one in charge.

"You know, you don't see dwarfs anymore, the way you used to," he said, once we were on the interstate. "I wonder what happened to them all." He sat back and put his sneakered feet up on the dash.

I'd thought I'd get the upper hand once we were alone, but though I felt a little less frightened, something else had kicked in, some kind of warped, low-frequency exhilaration. I didn't feel like myself, I felt twelve, I felt like Johnny Fever's girlfriend. The highway shimmered before me like ribbon candy. "What's your plan?" I asked, stealing glances at Gary's now-handsome face. "Back to your mother's?"

"I never went there," he said. "Hey, aren't you happy I brought Stevie Wonder? So you can work on your dissertation on the way."

"The way where?" I said.

"Are you kidding?" he said. "You really don't know? I always thought you were one step ahead of me on this kind of thing."

"*Where?*"

"It's your dream come true, baby. We're going to see the Cantankerous Judge!"

"What?"

"Hollywood!" he screamed. Outside, it thundered.

"What, you got studio-audience tickets?"

"No," he said. He sounded annoyed with me for asking. It began to rain, fat late-afternoon drops splatting egglike against the glass, and I searched with one hand for the wiper switch. "Oh, here," he finally said, reaching disgustedly over the steering column. The wipers came on. I saw exit signs for Marianna, Bonifay, Ponce de Leon. Soon would be Alabama, I knew, though I had only seen this stretch on maps.

"I'm sure we're going to make it all the way to California," I said. I was trying for indignance, my old exasperation, but I heard how silly and Valley Girl I sounded. Besides, there were no cops in sight.

Gary sang along with the stereo: *You ask me if I'm happy, well, as a matter of fact, I can say that I'm ecstatic, 'cause we both just made a pact* . . . It began to rain harder, horizontal sallies slicing rhythmically into the windshield, and I leaned forward, pushing the van through it as though trying to force my way into another dimension, another world.

"Where will we sleep?" I asked, after a while—a few minutes, or an hour.

"Don't worry about that, baby," Gary said. "I think this is a real turning point for us." He broke open a package of pistachios and began feeding them to me, cracking each nut and then pushing it gently between my lips.

Later we made love in the side lot of a Cracker Barrel, struggling to keep our heads down so no one would see. The van's vinyl floor corrugations cut into my back, and when I cried out, Gary put his salty, red-stained mouth on mine and murmured, "Speak not, child!"—what the Cantankerous Judge told people who tried to interrupt. I closed my eyes and easily, surprisingly, forgot where we were.

The clanging Dumpster woke us at dawn, the sky already bright and less forgiving, more distant-looking than it had been the day before. Gary said I was going to have to drive faster. Mississippi and Alabama were far behind, brief, briny-smelling memories, but Louisiana was making him nervous. The sooner we got out of this crazy state, he said, the better.

"I've got to eat and pee," I said. "That's only fair." I didn't have a plan, I was being honest. He assessed me for a long second and then nodded, and I let myself out and walked into the restaurant.

I was surprised that none of the customers or servers gave me a significant look or special message in the manner of the baseball-bat woman. An aproned employee brushed behind me at the restroom sink, where I was scrubbing off highway grime, but she never said a word. I could have asked for help then, but I was flustered by the way she stepped around me in the tiny cubicle, keeping her eyes down with almost religious determination. She didn't seem oblivious; rather, I got the unsettling impression that she knew exactly what was going on between me and Gary but was deliberately withholding her gaze. This was something new, I understood, an unfamiliar but higher level of signal than the kind I'd gotten in the past. Its meaning was not yet clear to me, but the overall implication was that I had certain choices, I would no longer be allowed certain excuses.

Gary had gotten us a table and plates of pancakes. "You look different," he said.

"Well, I washed my face."

"Something else."

"Well, I didn't get much sleep," I snapped.

"No, no," he said, "I meant you look good. Your eyes are more immediate, or something. Forget it." He sighed, took a large bite, and through it said, "We can go back if you're tired."

Our waitress arrived at that moment, white-bloused and hawk-faced, and I almost choked. She was the double of the baseball-bat woman, only minus the warmth, the seeping sympathy. She towered over us, glaring at me severely, ignoring Gary altogether, and I suddenly imagined she had

met with the woman from the bathroom regarding my cul-
pability—it seemed possible. "Anything else?" she finally
said. Her name tag read SHYTONIA.

"No, ma'am," I whispered.

"What was her problem?" Gary said, staring after her
fiercely retreating back.

I shook my head. "Can we just hurry?"

"Of course," he said. "We can do whatever you want. I
love you."

Back in the van, he drove and I held the machete. It was
heavier than I expected, with the ungainly, impractical
heft of a ceremonial object, and holding it made me begin
to feel better, reverent and a little festive. For his part, I
had to admit Gary looked better in the driver's seat than
I, preternaturally comfortable, as if the seat and perhaps
the whole vehicle were extensions of his body and his
powers. "They should never have fired you," I exclaimed,
and he cut his eyes at me and smiled, oozing certainty of
purpose.

Still, I knew we didn't have long. We were going faster,
and I had the sensation that something was rattling out of
us, our selves, perhaps, being whittled away and purified

by distance and speed. I kept catching myself glancing anxiously over my shoulder, expecting the lights and sirens at any moment. I wasn't irrational, I knew what awaited us. There would be officers and attorneys, paperwork, phone calls, and brief media coverage, and finally, by the time nobody cared anymore, a tedious hearing in our town's orange-and-turquoise-paneled courthouse, where the corridors smelled of fish sticks and cleaning fluid and the criminals all looked embarrassed. The judge, a gray-faced local, would speak without wrath or passion, deliver his decision in an uninspiring monotone, probation, probably, or a fine, thinking he was doing us and society a favor. And then we would be set free, sent away with neither wisdom nor forgiveness, nothing but ourselves to go home to.

I turned to Gary to tell him to floor it, but he was one step ahead of me, his jaw tight, fists gripping the wheel like he was piloting a rocket. I reached for the volume knob, turned up the music, tried to forget myself in the worried, forward-pushing beat, Wonder telling the world to keep on turning until we reached higher ground.

There was still a chance, I thought, no matter how slight,

that we'd actually make it—pull into Hollywood, find the studio, wait in whatever lines we had to, and then get our turn at last, stand before the Judge in person, not as audience members but as defendants. *Help us,* we'd beg, with whatever heart we had left, *please.*

Mr. Puniverse

YESTERDAY YOU SMELLED like detergent, having biked to work through the feeder bands of a tropical storm that was stalled just offshore in the Gulf, its center breaking up. You clomped in like a draft horse, keys and change jingling, clean shirt steaming sweet ammonia and dripping all over the linoleum in the Xerox room, arms loaded with souvenirs from your recent vacation in a Midwestern state you refused to name: "A Midwestern state of mind," was all you would say.

To the reporters and editors, you presented trial-size jars of specialty barbecue sauce: Macintosh-smoked, Jack-Daniel's-spiked, Ginseng Zinger, Grand Marnier Infusion.

The custodial staff got a box of chocolates shaped like prairie dogs. For Mabel, the front-desk receptionist, a postcard of the famous fainting goats. For Kenny and Sonny, the other two photographers besides myself, car air-fresheners in the shape of the anonymous Midwestern state. Kenny said he'd take Sonny's to him in the hospital. "Oh, yes, that's right," you said, your eyes meeting no one's.

After you had given everything out, you turned to me. My empty hands vibrated in anticipation—something was finally going to pass between us. Like a goat, I thought I might faint.

"I'm still working on yours," you said. Your tone was both secretive and ironic, I thought, a little anxious but also triumphant, frustrated but resolute—sincere, yet more than a little recalcitrant.

"Is something wrong?" I said.

"Ha!" you laughed, throwing back your large wet head, sending out an arc of storm-charged droplets. I watched one hit the bulletin board behind you and blur the word "operations" on a memo. The fluorescents flickered, went out, then blinked back on. "Whoa!" someone in the next room shouted.

"You just look a little anxious," I said. "Or, not anxious —worried. Worried."

Your hand moved across your gray-cratered chin, making an amplified, space-age sound. You said, "Well, it takes a worried man to sing a worried song." And then, backing away as if I had stepped too close, though I hadn't moved or even swallowed: "I'll try to bring yours tomorrow. Yours is special."

A wave of something went through me, tweaked my hyped-up aminos. I saw fish leaping out of the sea before a tsunami, strange fuzzy tendrils pushed out of the ground by the shifting plates of the earth. It didn't matter what the gift was. I could feel everything that was happening everywhere, and it was all for me.

MY FIRST PHOTO shoot for the paper was the Mr. Puniverse Pageant, in which the editors had jokingly entered you, their colleague, as a contestant. I hadn't met you yet, but everyone was abuzz about the event, the fact that you were going along with it. "And Jason, you're the perfect man to cover this," the editors said to me, with genuine, mean-spirited excitement. "You'll make these dorks feel even more puny, get some great reactions." They were a giggling, sweaty, vengeful group, these editors. They reminded me to get some good shots of you for the bulletin board. "You'll know him, he'll be the *old* one!" they hooted.

Twenty years their—and your—junior, I had my killer summer tan, still, and was experimenting with a black-market protein powder that had doubled my muscle mass in a month and was probably veterinary steroids, which was fine with me. Smells and sounds were more intense, people got on my nerves more, but I was buff, I was ripped. I had no idea who you were. "Sure," I told the editors. "Whatever."

You did not win the title of Mr. Puniverse, didn't even place—while comically homely, certainly, you were not particularly skinny. Really, you didn't even make an effort. For your talent segment, you told one joke: "What's a potato's favorite TV show? *M*A*S*H*." The reporters from our paper cheered wildly.

Still, I found it hard to look away from you, to pay attention to the proceedings. You were scuffing around the margins of the stage, absently stepping in and out of your sandals, keeping your eyes down, occasionally glancing up to grin at someone jeering at you from the audience. Your gaze at those moments I found staggering. Clapton was playing on the PA—*I've seen some dark skies, never like this, walked on some thin ice, never like this*—and the maddening, animal smell of barbecue from the concession stand was rolling over me in waves. When I tried to take your picture, the power suddenly drained from my camera, and the shutter wouldn't budge. Luckily, I'd brought a backup camera.

The winner, the new Mr. Puniverse, was an albino biologist named Bultinck who stood six-two and weighed 111. In the interview we printed, he said, "I breed genetically specific mice, for which there is a pretty steady demand. I'm used to people thinking I'm weird." Energized by your presence, I got an inspired portrait of him, a happy freak naked from the waist up, the cold metal of the trophy he clutched making his nipples pop out. His figure appeared to be outlined in light, or hope, coming from some outside source.

Afterward, I pushed backstage, that song still playing in my head—*I've told some white lies, never like this, looked into true eyes, never like this*—and offered you a ride back to the office in what I hoped was a neutral, businesslike tone. My parking meter, when we reached it, had apparently broken—in digital letters its screen said JAR. "Jar," you repeated, looking at me. I thought: *My god, your eyes.* Together, elbows knocking, we slid your Schwinn, a ladies' one-speed, into my backseat. I could hear the atoms in the cracks of space between us going crazy, buzzing like angry gnats.

Later, when I asked if you were bummed about losing the pageant, you said, "You can't always get what you want," and then gave me a look of nearly hysterical satisfaction. I would learn it was your habit to work popular song lyrics into your conversation whenever possible with a kind of feverish, driven desperation, as if they were being pumped into you via secret radio waves and this was the only way to get them out of your system.

In fact, one question I frequently found myself wanting to ask you, later, was: "Didn't the electroconvulsive shock therapy help with the loose association?" But I would die before I'd remind you of something that hurt you.

Though you yourself never spoke of it, everyone at the paper knew and told a different version of your troubled youth and unjust incarceration in a state mental institution, your close brush with and lucky reprieve from lobotomy. In one version you had simply been a difficult teenager—for a year you refused to eat anything but Necco wafers, refused to read anything but the Fantasy Baseball Index, and in your free time sneaked out of the house and climbed electrical towers. What choice did your affluent, dim-witted, Eisenhower-voting-for parents have but to commit you?

In another version you tried to kill your father with a fencing foil. I found that version hard to believe, not because I couldn't imagine you as murderous, but because, in your own discordant, distracted, disintegrating way, you had too much style, too much real dignity for anything as idiotically self-important as fencing. You would have used your bare hands, I believed, or any simple firearm.

The length of your stay in the place, three years, was common knowledge. Your parents moved across country for your father's promotion, so you had to wait until you turned eighteen to sign yourself out. Office consensus was that you had come out crazier than you had gone in, and this unusual bit of generosity on the part of your otherwise relentlessly critical colleagues—that they would grant you this—was, I thought, a measure of your personal power, your grace. It made my heart swell, like that of some idiot housewife, to think of it.

Never were they as hushed and reverent as when they

spoke of your electroshock, how it made you smell roses even in your sleep, and see people as cartoons, how it made your thoughts seem to come from a space like a luggage compartment located in the air ten feet above your head, how it made you forget your own name. I thought it must also have been the reason for your eyes—the layered, flickering darkness, the look, at one instant, of both reaching and refraining from reaching.

I couldn't think about it without the edges of my own body starting to crackle, tingle, not in sympathy, but with the urge to hurl itself back through time and take your body's place, get between you and the source of the shocks, let the electricity mess with my simple, unspecial brain, my not-fragile self. I could have withstood it, I was sure, especially now with my new bulk. What good were my youth and strength doing anyone here, now? If only I had been there, I wanted to tell you, believe me, you would have come to no harm. Over my dead body.

That night, after the Mr. Puniverse Pageant, I dreamed I broke your bike. An accident—I was riding it, showing off for you, and the brake levers came off in my hands. The next night I dreamed that, together, you and I broke my TV, simply by standing in a certain proximity to each other and looking at it. In the dream, I understood that the TV was a sacrifice: if I didn't get to touch you, it was I who might die.

SONNY THE SENIOR photographer quickly noticed me noticing you, and made sure I noticed. He caught me in the men's room, pulled me aside from nothing in particular, and said, "*By the way,* he's not gay," in an obnoxiously pointed, fake-offhand manner, stroking his pubic-looking goatee with his ratty, precise little hand. Sonny Von Cher, I called him to my friends. Straight photographers were, in my experience, a bunch of assholes, constantly needing to prove that they were discerning hidden aspects of things, making it their life's work to unearth and destroy faith wherever they found it. Sonny was always pointing out examples of "unusual beauty" in a pompous, spiteful manner, as though he alone possessed the special powers to recognize it, as though the rest of us, the masses, were too stupid and insensitive to appreciate or even know the real thing when we saw it.

Still, he had made his point. I brought it up on the way to Disney Gay Day with Owen, Kirk, Remy, Heath, Germain, Tab, Fidel, and Eddie, in the Aerostar we had all chipped in to rent for the weekend.

"Why does Sonny care if you like this old ugly crazy straight guy?" Eddie said. "Does he want him?"

"No, Sonny's got a girlfriend," I said. "Though she does look like a boy. Or a praying mantis."

"Wait!" Owen yelled. "This guy you're in love with is old *and* straight *and* ugly? Maybe *you're* the one who's not gay!"

"He's not ugly *per se,*" I said.

"He's not ugly, he's per se," Tab said.

"He's not ugly, he's my brother," Germain said.

"I'm telling you," I said. "I just have this feeling . . ."

"Oh, please. Wake me up when we get to the Magic Kingdom."

As usual, Kirk was the only one who would take me seriously. We were lying in the back with the luggage, watching the string of sulphur-pink streetlights snaking by in the sky. "Sometimes," Kirk said, "wanting what you can never have is the perfect spiritual position. Your faith develops, becomes an entity unto itself, takes on nearly physical reality. Like the relationship we have with the dead, how the dead can sometimes seem more present than the living. Loving an absent partner is beautiful."

"It's not beautiful, it's pathetic," Remy said, leaning over his seat. "The guy is straight, listen to what Sonny says. Forget about it."

"Who cares what Soon-Yi says," Kirk said. "That doesn't mean anything."

"Maybe he is straight," I said, "but there's this look he gives me that just—I can't explain it."

"Communion," Kirk said.

"Spare me the Touched-by-an-Angel crap, will you?" Remy said. "Don't you remember what happened last year when Fidel hooked up with that 'bisexual' cardiac nurse guy?"

"Cancer care," Fidel said.

"Whatever. I personally don't have the time right now to sit up all night through Jason's nervous breakdown caused by some old freak who isn't even attractive."

"Okay, we won't call you," Kirk said. "God, Remy, you're like, Touched by an Asshole. You think you're everything."

"I *am* everything," Remy said. "I'm *it*."

Your image swam down to me from between the lights, flashed into me like a thought coming from ten feet above my head. I saw you again on the Mr. Puniverse stage, how you pulsed against my eyes as if you had been drawn in some darker, heavier medium than the other contestants, some radioactive kind of crayon. How you seemed the photographic negative of the boring joke that was being perpetuated there, and most other places, most of the time. How it hit me all at once that you were beautiful thinly disguised as ugly, the truth seeping out around your eyes and the vibrating edges of your person, the direct opposite of everyone else there, of most people I'd ever known, including, probably, myself.

Was I wrong, now, to believe you were taking a special interest in me? I thought of the way you stopped dead whenever we encountered each other in the corridor, and held up your hands in a gesture of surrender; the way you spoke just a bit more loudly whenever I was working nearby, as if we were animals who had to track each other by sound. The way you sometimes appeared outside the darkroom, said my name, "Jason—," but then nothing else, just stood there rubbing your chin, your eyes both bright and veiled, as if you were trying to remember the rest of the sentence.

"Besides," Kirk was saying, "Jason isn't having a nervous breakdown. Look at him, *hello,* he looks great. What have you been doing, Jason, lifting weights again? Your arms look bigger. Don't his arms look bigger? Look at his arms. Is it just me, or are your arms getting bigger? Jason?"

EVERYTHING I TOUCHED or even glanced at began to suffer mysterious surges and drains. Bulbs blew in every room of my apartment, and the coil on my toaster oven went cold. My water pressure fluctuated violently. New shoelaces snapped between my fingers; ink pens burst, unprovoked, in my pockets and desk drawers. My TV changed channels by itself, and my stereo suddenly picked up stations I'd never heard of, transmitting from cities hundreds of miles away. Downtown one day, a transformer I happened to walk by exploded, splattering the sidewalk behind me with hot oil. True, my body was growing so rapidly that I was bumping into things like an adolescent, having to adjust my conception of physical space. But I suspected something else at work, something that had visited me once before.

During one weekend when I was sixteen, I remembered, the year I was coming out, the compressor in my mother's meat freezer, my Sunbird's alternator, and my Swatch battery had all suddenly and mysteriously died. Then our answering machine, which otherwise worked fine, stopped taking messages from Kim Falvey, the girl I was dating. Clearly, it was trying to help me. Some enormous invisible presence seemed very close to me then, bearing terrifyingly down, ripping out what I pictured as notebook subject dividers in my brain. It peaked one night, and I made my parents kneel on the floor of my bedroom with me and pray, which they did without asking questions. They were good parents.

Kirk, whose father was a Masonic Perfect Master of the Fifth Degree, was actually hallucinating when he finally came out. On the way to school one morning, he said, he saw a giant hairball driving a truck. To escape his family, finally, he wrote a letter to himself from an imaginary friend, Lance, in Pecos, Texas, inviting himself to come visit for the summer, but his hallucinations had become so convincing by then that he was devastated when he stepped off the Greyhound and Lance wasn't there to meet him.

"There's a proven link between repression and increased electrical activity," Kirk said while we were waiting in line for Space Mountain. "How do you think a lie detector test works? So, the longer you hold it in, the worse it's going to get. Now on top of that, you say this guy had electroshock.

Very likely his altered electromagnetic field is messing up your gaydar. Add to that your own increased chemical conductivity caused by the, ahem, 'protein supplement' you're taking, and interactive aberration seems inevitable."

"That sounds plausible, Kirk," I said, "but with all these environmental variables, how can anyone tell who they're in love with, or who's in love with them?"

"It's in his kiss," Kirk said.

"Thanks," I said.

"Look," Kirk said, speaking more loudly. "This much I know. This is fact, recorded history. The pendulum clock in the palace of Frederick the Great at Sans Souci stopped when the emperor died. Whatever's causing all this to happen, this force, or whatever it is, this wave, or frequency, this configuration of light and heat and matter, this juxtaposition of events and possibilities, this *thing*. Whatever it is—it's trying to help you! You just have to have faith in it!" He had his hands on my shoulders and was yelling into my face. A jet roared right overhead then, so low it lifted my hair, and I stared up at its glaring silver underside, which appeared to be smiling at us. A moment later it was gone. Kirk looked worried. He said, "You saw that, too, right?"

• • •

I WANTED TO CONFESS, to tell you everything, but there was never the opportunity; Sonny, it had become clear, was trying to keep us apart. He gave me the most distant, time-consuming assignments—the WHIP 102-FM Chevy Touch-A-Thon, the grand opening of the Hair Shanty two counties away—so I'd be out of the office all day. When I returned, after dark, you were always gone. And then you took your Midwestern vacation. The day after you left, the tropical depression pulled up to the mainland and parked there, a perpetual-motion machine churning out storm after storm, as if the world itself had stalled, as if change were no longer possible. It seemed I might never see you again—an unacceptable ending.

Kenny guffawed one morning when I told him where Sonny was sending me, to photograph the renegade airport emu. "Let me tell you something, bro," he said. "No one's ever even *seen* that runaway ostrich. It's like a UFO, man."

My faith faltered, I'm sorry to say. I had to do something.

I caught Sonny in his cubicle, using a magnifying glass to scrutinize headshots of his Dilton-Doiley-looking girlfriend, and told him I needed his help. Rain was lashing the windows in ten-minute bursts, and I'd timed myself to ar-

rive between them, during one of the eerie, swollen silences, thinking I'd be more likely to get Sonny to go along
with me that way—I'd be in the flow, riding the waves of
air pressure like a surfer, coasting in to the inevitable end.
In the men's room mirror I'd made my face pleasant, expectant, like Mary Tyler Moore's normal expression. I only
hoped that suppressing my intentions wouldn't cause a
blackout or explosion before I had the chance to carry
them out.

"I'm having the damnedest time finding that emu," I
said. "I need the benefit of your expertise."

Sonny laughed. "You want me to go out in this storm?"

"I'm going. Besides, I thought you said it came out when
planes were grounded," I said. "Unless, you know, there is
no emu . . ."

"Oh, there's an emu," Sonny said. "I'll ride out on the
tarmac with you, how's that? Show you where it nests. I've
gotta go pick up my new lens anyway. But then you're on
your own, bud. You're still the new guy, in case you've
forgotten."

"Oh, no, never," I said. "Believe me, I feel fortunate."

In my car, he lit a cigarette and said, "You really need to
get over this little crush on our Mr. Puniverse."

Something clanged in the engine. *Easy,* I thought. *Just hang on a little longer.* I said, "Sorry?"

"Come on, Jason, spare me."

"Well, we've become friendly," I said. "If that's what you mean."

"He's an interesting guy," Sonny said, his tone implying that he knew everything about you, and I knew nothing. "His father was editor in chief, years ago. Dead now. So we try to look out for him. Keep him out of trouble."

"And?"

"And so the last thing he needs—or the paper needs—is a gay stalker. Where's your ashtray?" Water slammed the passenger half of the windshield, as though aiming for him. "Hey, slow down," he said, "will you?"

"Sorry," I said. We were on the long, pine-lined entranceway to the terminal, a single supermarket-sized building, and the open sky over the runways was visible, striped with wide dark bands, like the shadows of giant fan blades moving in slow motion. I couldn't get there fast enough.

"Turn here behind the rental cars," Sonny said. "It'll take us right out on the tarmac. I hope you've been paying attention to what I've said. I don't care what you do at home, behind closed doors, but I hope you're listening to me. We had forty-five applicants for your position."

"You want to protect him from me," I said, steering to where he was pointing. "Right? *You* want to protect *him* from *me*." I cut the engine and it knocked twice, some thunder rumbling along with it. We were at the edge of the gate's concrete skirting, facing out on the empty runways, and beyond them the thick stands of longleaf pine and palmetto scrub, from which the bird would supposedly emerge. A lone prop jet sat at the gate, unattended. I pulled my camera bag from the backseat, pretended to rummage in it. There was the little gun Owen had lent me—shiny, pretty.

"I'd watch the sarcasm if I were you," Sonny said.

"Watch the birdie, watch the sarcasm," I said. Blood rushed and beat in my ears, building in tempo. Sonny was glaring at me, stroking his scraggly chin, and it occurred to me that he might be sneakily appropriating your gestures, one by one, even as he proclaimed himself your protector.

"Look, it's let up," he said finally. "Let's get out there, okay? I don't have all day."

We marched along single-file in the drenched grass, parallel to the treeline, his black-jeaned butt twitching self-righteously in front of me. The words I planned to say hurtled through my head. "You didn't come this far last time, did you?" he said.

"I could never have come this far without you," I said.

"Okay," he said, stopping and brushing his hands together, as though he'd just finished a dirty job. "I'm out of here. I'll grab a cab, and why don't you just not come back in at all, okay?"

"I'm sorry," I said. "I don't think I understand." Thunder boomed as the next band of dark moved in.

Sonny glanced at the sky, then down at his shirtfront, which was beginning to speckle. "Look, I don't want some kind of showdown," he said. "Why don't you just do the honorable thing, the graceful thing—"

"Graceful!" I said. "This is a showdown." It was time. "This is a showdown about beauty," I began, but he had already turned his back and was heading for the terminal, his feet slapping into a jog. "Wait!" I yelled. "You fucking coward!" The wind had picked up and I didn't think he heard me. *You are the enemy of beauty,* I was going to say. *If beauty is to survive, you must be destroyed.* I broke into a run behind him, not to catch up, as I knew he couldn't match me for speed, but because the storm was suddenly enormous, almost upon us. Funny, I thought, it sounds like a locomotive.

Something huge and black and silver was bearing down, crackling and roaring like a metallic bear, moving faster than both of us. *You!* I thought, returning from your vacation just in time—but the planes weren't flying, and you weren't due back until the next day. Still, I knew it was going to help me, and I tilted my head back to greet it, grateful, relieved—I wouldn't need the gun. There was a pause in the noise, like an intake of breath, and then the lightning smacked down a few yards in front of me, knocking Sonny sideways. His body seemed to hang in the air for a moment, as the charge exited it, and then it folded and fell, almost slowly, like a used-up helium balloon, making no sound when it hit the ground. "Thank you," I said, out loud.

The light had gone back up in the sky and was pulsing on and off there, a signal meant just for me. Rain sliced down finally. I heard the sirens start back at the terminal— the trucks would reach us in seconds, I knew, so I didn't have to do anything, nothing was required of me. I stood there with my hands dangling, like a beautiful girl, helpless, guiltless, perfect.

Before the authorities could get there, though, a figure

crashed out of the trees beside Sonny's body, a shape moving tentatively, then quickly toward me, tall and impossibly skinny and outlined in light, a familiar silhouette. *Bultinck?* I whispered. But it whooshed right past, feathers rustling, the smell of burned flesh and roses fluttering in the air behind it.

MR. MEEK

ONE OF THE THREE girl crack addicts Terry's boss had hired told Terry there was a man in town giving away money. Terry laughed and tried to ignore her. He knew Jill from the bars—everyone did—and didn't take her seriously—no one did. Her lies were indiscriminate and hysterical, like *Ripley's Believe It or Not*: "You know, there's a guy in Texas who counterfeited a million-dollar bill and got away with it," she'd say, or, "You know you can die from eating glitter?" She looked anorexic and about ten, with chlorine-scorched pigtails, until you got up close and saw her face, carved with walnut lines. But she always found some guy to take her in, some poor doormat who didn't know her yet, who would brag for a couple weeks that she was sleeping in his guest room, getting her GED, thanks to him she was getting it together. Then suddenly she'd be back at the bars, dragging her shopping bags of mismatched clothes and mildewed carnival-prize stuffed animals. She spooked Terry—her eyes had the high-frequency sparkle of a dog smelling fear at fifty yards. He suspected it was only a matter of time before she tried to hit him up for something.

"Nobody gives away money," he told her. He punched his time card and buckled on his lifting belt, keeping his back to her and the other two crack addicts.

Jill imitated the man, dropping her voice. "He says, *If they don't ask, I give it to them. If they ask, I don't give it to them.*"

"Sounds like an asshole," Terry said.

"You wouldn't say that if he gave you a hundred bucks," she said. "He was at Wal-Mart yesterday, I'm not kidding, just standing by the checkout, picking out people to pay for. Said his name was Mr. Meek, from Corpus Christi, and he's here to *share the wealth*. Wouldn't say how long he's planning to stay or nothing, just *share the wealth*."

Besides the fact he didn't believe her, Terry hated when

people told you about something lucky you'd missed—how
dumb was that? He would have preferred not to talk to the
crack girls at all—all three of them were watching him now,
waiting for his reaction—but the only way to the warehouse was through the front room, where they sat at a table
assembling circuit boards. The other two, Helen and Mo,
were less canny and starved-seeming than Jill, but they still
depressed him. Helen was fat, claimed to cast spells on the
barmaids when they cut her off, and gave blow jobs in the
bars' parking lots. Mo, an upbeat, jockish lesbian, glowed
improbably with good health and always said she was doing "super," though she frequently got arrested for shoplift-
ing groceries and phoned around to the bars for someone to
bail her out. No one knew where Helen and Mo lived—
wherever crack addicts lived, Terry supposed—but at least
they never asked to stay with anyone.

No one could believe it when Alan hired them, but that
was Alan, always helping somebody. And the arrangement
had worked for several months now, no problem with the
girls except how uncomfortable they made Terry, but he
was certainly in no position to complain, and no one else
seemed to find their presence as unsettling as he did. The
girls' assembly job required neither special knowledge nor

steady hands. "This is easy, like Lite Brite," Jill said on her first day, beaming her black-holed grin, "only it don't light up."

"My *dog* could do that job," Alan joked. Alan's scruffy chow—a pound dog, of course, damaged in some mysterious way by its previous owners—sat dead-still for hours in the parking lot all day, staring straight up in the air at nothing anyone could see, barking endlessly like a broken machine, *Urt-urt-urt-urt-urt.*

"If you don't believe me, watch the news!" Jill shouted at Terry now. "*Mr. Meek,* he was on the news!"

"Calm down, I believe you," Terry said. "What is he, like that coin guy who came down from Nashville? Who told everyone whatever they had was worthless? Hey, if you want to wait in line for three hours to be told you're worthless, that's your right." Terry remembered the photos in the paper, the long line of pathetic, hopeful faces, tightly clutched baggies and cigar boxes and coffee cans, each person thinking he was the one, the exception that would prove the rule. In the end, no one had anything worth anything, and the coin guy looked smug, like he had known it all along.

"Mine wouldn't of been worthless except I washed it," Jill said. "He said nobody wants a clean coin."

"Alan told us when he was a kid he used to eat coins," Mo said. "That's how much he loved money. He always knew he was going to make it."

"Numismatist, that's what that Nashville guy was," Helen said, her fat hands working away.

"Wasn't no numismatist, he was just an asshole," Mo said. "But listen, Terry, Jill's telling the truth, this guy really is giving away money. He's paying for folks' groceries. He was at *my* Winn-Dixie last night, only I ain't allowed in there anymore, how's that! How am I supposed to share the wealth if I ain't even allowed in the store?"

"Guess what, you had your chance and you blew it," Terry said, finally pushing out the steel door. In the corner of his eye he caught Mo's stuck-out tongue, and he wondered how it could still appear so pink and normal. You'd think addicts' tongues would turn black, like Alan's dog's tongue, or shrivel up or something.

The warehouse guys were planning to position themselves at every grocery store in town—"full zone coverage," they called it. Then they'd split the winnings, like with a lottery ticket. "Although what are we gonna do with all them extra groceries?" a little sawed-off guy named Tommy said.

"You got a point," someone else said. "But if they're free, hey."

"No, I mean the ones that *ain't* free," Tommy said.

"Man, I am sick of listening to this bullshit," Terry said. He barely spoke aloud—just under his breath as he dragged a pallet—but several guys stopped what they were doing and stared.

"What the hell's your problem?" one of them said.

"Man, no kidding, lighten up," Tommy said. "We're all in the same boat."

"Speak for yourself," Terry said, half-hoping to start a fight. But no one ever took him seriously; at twenty-one he was the youngest guy there, no old lady, no kids, in their minds just a baby. *You ain't even lived yet,* they told him. *You ain't seen nothing.* He didn't bother to correct them.

At break he went back to Alan's glassed-in office to ask for time off, which he knew he would get. He took a long weekend each month to drive up to his sister's in Atlanta, ever since her boy, his nephew, aged five, had died last summer. A pitched ball had hit Chase in the chest at a game and made his heart stop. *Freak accident,* every single person who ever heard about it said. Like saying "Bless you" to a sneeze—Terry had never heard so many people say the same useless thing. Alan, at least, always urged Terry to take more days off, as many as he needed. "Jesus," he said when Terry first told him. "There are some things worth dying for, but, man, Little League ain't one of them."

Alan was self-made, a genius, and, everyone said, a saint. He built amplifiers, envisioned or sometimes even dreamed their circuitry, new ways of connecting wires that would produce unearthly treble, seismic bass. He'd started Alan's Amps single-handedly—*literally*, he joked: he was missing his left arm, from having let a blood clot go too long. Another joke he always made when he passed out paychecks was: *One hand giveth, and the other taketh away.* He seemed not to mind his disability, and often removed his expensive prosthesis before meeting with buyers, landing him monster sales, he claimed. When he was bored or depressed he amused himself by trying to build the world's smallest amplifier, and his efforts, the prototypes, sat in a display case in the company showroom, intricate, enigmatic little silver-and-black contraptions, completely impractical yet strangely powerful and impressive, like diamonds.

Terry didn't think Alan was a saint, and he knew Alan didn't think so either—when someone called him one he answered, "I ain't no saint." He was just smart, with a perverse generous streak fueled by guilt, Terry thought. Alan felt guilty because his wife had killed herself, years ago. Everyone knew the story—Terry couldn't remember who he'd heard it from—but nobody talked about it in front of Alan. It was after the suicide, supposedly, that he'd let his arm go, like a sacrifice, and Terry figured it was also why he took pity on the addicts, the dog—and probably, for that matter, on Terry himself, though Terry hated to think of himself lumped together with the girls in Alan's mind.

Still, Terry was grateful. Alan had hired him on for summer, car-stereo season, but then let him stay when he decided not to go back to community college in the fall. He'd picked classes, registered, and paid, but then at the last moment just couldn't go. Instead, he dozed on his plaid sofa, traveled only between the most recently familiar places— the warehouse, the bars, home—as if the forward-moving mechanism of his life had stalled, stopped at the same moment as Chase's heart.

What was he waiting for? An explanation to come in the mail? Unlike his sister, he wasn't obsessed with restitution.

He didn't fantasize, like she did, that Chase would return someday, ring the doorbell accompanied by some Technicolor TV version of an angel. When he was growing up, his sister's life had seemed a reassuring preview of his own— but now it was like a small, awful map with his name on it, one he wished he'd never seen. Only at work, where nobody but Alan knew about Chase, could he momentarily escape, obliterate himself.

The images still came to him in the afternoons, though, as he lifted and hauled, cranking the familiar mesh of his muscles. He saw Chase's white belly bobbing in fake-blue pool water, his own big hand under the boy's back, holding him afloat. The weird, charged feel of the little torso, its slight weight rendered incidental by the water, yet so obviously, mysteriously alive. So that if you were blindfolded, supporting two bodies, one with each hand, you would know: *This one's alive.* He saw Chase's twitchy hands, stained by Magic Markers, which the boy said he hated because you could never feel them touch you until it was too late and your skin was already all marked up.

The week after Chase's funeral a girl Terry was dating took him to a private beach near St. Augustine, where they watched a group of sea turtle hatchlings stagger en masse from their fenced nests into the ocean's foam line—though only five percent would survive, a volunteer explained. They all looked the same, Terry thought. He felt his rage rise unaccountably. What was the point of hatching turtles if you were just going to send them out into the wild to get killed?

Rather than get into it with the girl, he kept his mouth shut and then just quit calling her. It occurred to him that the turtles were not going to be an isolated incident, that from now on there would be a lot of things that would piss him off, that he could no longer enjoy, and he wouldn't know what they were until they were upon him. Alan had once described how, even years after his arm was gone, he still came up against unexpected ways he'd used it, movements he'd taken for granted that were now lost to him. Terry saw himself stumbling through the rest of his days, trying to negotiate the empty space Chase had left. And to figure out exactly what part of himself was missing—what part of the self or life a nephew occupied, a boy you didn't even see that often, or think that much about one way or the other, until he was gone, and then it turned out he had been everywhere all along. So that now he kept popping up in every corner of your existence, handicapping everything, demanding to be recognized, remembered, explained.

He phoned his sister from the bar so he could use the noise as an excuse not to hear her. She had done the same to him when Chase was alive, practicing the right of parental selective hearing. "Hold on, hold on, Mommy's on the phone —" she'd say, suddenly, psychically letting Chase pull her away whenever Terry was about to ask for money or spill his guts about some girl.

Now he let these drunks pull him away from his sister's tiny, aching voice. Jill was there, begging quarters for the jukebox, so she could play "I Feel the Earth Move Under My Feet," or whatever the hell that song was called, over and over, like she always did, until the barmaids finally cut off the power, making everyone swear, hands in the air, not to play that song again, before they'd turn it back on.

"I got the paperwork on that liability insurance . . ." his sister's voice was saying, like a fishhook in his ear.

Jill swam toward him, palm outstretched, her backlit outline skeletal, and behind her, Alan gestured frantically from his barstool, making a throat-cutting motion and mouthing, *No more, no more,* the gesture seeming more emphatic somehow because he made it with his one arm. "Well, I'll be there tomorrow by suppertime," Terry said into the phone.

"You already said that," his sister said. "Listen—"

Jill had him against the wall, her fist twisting in his pocket, knuckles hard against his hipbone. Tommy came over then and tugged her off, but she waved her handful of coins in the air triumphantly. "I love you, Terry!" she called.

His sister was crying. "You don't give a shit," she said.

"Come on," he said. "You know that's not true." It was getting harder, though. Last time he visited, she showed him a folder of photos she'd printed out off the Internet, faces of strangers, technologically age-progressed. This was what they did if your child got kidnapped, she told him. Each pair of photos had a *before,* the actual child in a school or department-store wallet shot—something off-key about all their look-alike, innocent grins, as though the knowledge of their fate was contained somewhere therein—and an *after,* what they would look like now, four, seven, ten years later, their new, constructed smiles artificially lit, *like Lite Brite,* Terry thought. For five hundred dollars they could do Chase, his sister explained excitedly, make a new composite each year, show him any age she wanted. This is too fucking weird for me, Terry said, and she exploded at him, *You don't understand, you don't understand!*

He dreaded going to see her anymore. At the beginning he'd helped keep things under control when her ex, Chase's father, showed up to exchange accusations, all of them on both sides beginning with *If you hadn't —*, as though if they could just determine the source, the original sin, they would understand why the accident had happened, or why it had happened to them. Now, though, there was nothing left for Terry to take care of, nothing he could do. And she looked at him so hungrily, as if he were carrying traces of Chase on his person, hiding them from her, cheating her by still being alive.

Jill was there with a beer when he hung up, and he needed it so he took it. "Why the generosity?" he said.

"I heard about your little brother," she said hoarsely. "I'm real sorry." She watched him react, then said, "Don't worry, I didn't tell nobody."

He opened his mouth to correct her, then shut it quickly. He felt something physical, like Chase's life, leaking out of the world. A belated, bodily urge to protect the boy plagued him in spasms, like dry heaves. He didn't want any part of Chase, even his name, brought into this bar. He wished he could take her words out of the air.

"Alan said you didn't want no one to know," she said.

"Why the hell did he tell you then?"

"I'm staying at his house," she said.

"Wow, he really is a saint." He was trying for sarcasm, something to put her off, but as he spoke he realized that would be impossible, like trying to break something already broken, or injure a punching bag. Anyway, he was surprised; he thought Alan would have known better.

Jill made a scornful face. "Saint, my ass. I'm doing him a favor. That man is desperate for a woman. After his wife, what she did, and then that stump of his? Who wants to look at that? I'll tell you what, he smells like a big Band-Aid. Disgusting. We all feel sorry for him."

"You all?"

"Me and Helen and Mo. For a while there we was all living there at once, all sleeping in his *bed*, now that was wild," she said. "Alan's Angels, he called us. I'm the only one lasted more than a week."

He winced, trying not to picture it, and glanced at Alan sitting royally there at the bar, his false hand on someone's back, buying drinks for everybody. "I don't believe you," he said. "Mo's not even straight."

"Yeah, she was, that night. But now she lives in mini-storage. Don't tell anyone. It ain't legal."

Mini-storage. He recalled the flimsy-looking white shelters set up over the sea turtles' nests, like a bunch of Chinese take-out cartons on the sand. And Chase's half-sized casket.

"Helen's the only one who wouldn't make it with him," Jill said. "You know how she is: *I don't need any man.*"

Terry pressed the sweating bottle against his temple and shut his eyes. In his mind he saw a giant, damp tumbleweed of people, a gray, pity-and-lust-saturated knot from which it was impossible to disentangle the strong from the weak, helper from helped, who owed whom. And Alan's benevolent face in the middle of it, urging Terry to jump in—like he'd done as a boy, diving into playground fights, hanging back for two seconds to make sure no teacher was watching, and then the release, the joyous loss in the scramble of bodies where limbs and blame were indistinguishable, *Nobody's fault, nobody's fault* . . . Well, he wasn't even tempted. Chase was there, ever present now, floating above them all, untethered and pure as a star, determining everything. Unreachable, inescapable.

"Jesus," he said, opening his eyes. "What the hell are you wearing, anyway?" Jill had on what appeared to be an actual children's dress, pink and flouncy, over spandex bicycle shorts that bagged on her bony legs. She stepped toward him, taking his attention as an invitation, and pushed her face grotesquely close.

"You want to meet Mr. Meek," she said. "I know where he's at. You look so sad, I'll bet he gives you something."

"Thanks for the beer, gotta go," he said. She snagged his T-shirt sleeve.

"I'm not lying," she said. "I met him! I know where he's at right now."

"What makes you think I give a shit where he's at?"

"Give me a ride and I'll tell you."

"Come on, Jill, lay off."

"Alan built a sound system for him, I'm not lying! Come on, please, just drop me off at Food Folks. I won't tell anyone about your brother, I promise."

What the hell, he thought, everyone at work gave Jill a ride sooner or later—like paying dues, and then, he hoped, with her unfailing knack for knowing just how much she could take from each person, she'd move on to somebody else. "All right," he said grimly. She shrieked and tried to hug him, but he shimmied out of her grasp. "You keep your mouth shut," he said, "about—" Chase's name wouldn't say itself out loud. She nodded as if she'd heard him, though, as if speech and thoughts were all the same to her.

He slammed his empty on the bar by Alan's good elbow, refusing to answer Alan's fake-innocent, questioning look— Alan, whom he had admired. Tommy was propping open the door with a pool cue. "I knew it was just a matter of time before you two got together," he said to Terry and Jill.

"Yeah, you know everything," Terry said. He kicked the cue out of Tommy's hand, people turning their heads at the clatter, but Tommy just laughed.

Jill crouched between two trucks the second she got outside, and curled her shoulders around a thermometer-shaped pipe. Terry yelled for her to hurry up, but she was gone, winnowed down to that dot of orange light, a string of smoke unfurling up into the sky.

When she climbed in his Honda she wasn't hyped, as he expected, but diluted, scattered and distant, like animals let out of a pen, run to the farthest edges of a field. He had read somewhere that crack was getting weaker, not what it used to be. But this stuff must've done its job—she looked like a well-behaved ghost of herself. It unsettled him, and he peeled out quickly. "I don't care if you don't believe me," she mumbled.

"What are you talking about?" He didn't care, he just wanted to keep her conscious. He hoped, too late now, of course, that his taillight wasn't out, or his plates expired. He didn't think it was possible to catch a buzz off her breath in the closed car, but he cranked down his window just in case.

"Mr. *Meek*," she said. "He's going to give me something, he promised."

"Yeah, right," he snorted. "If Mr. Meek gave you a *dime*, I'd eat my hat."

"Ha," she said. "I'm gonna win that one."

"If, number one, this guy actually exists, and number two, he gives you *anything*, I will personally pay you a hundred dollars," Terry said. "And kick his ass," he added.

He felt and almost heard her spark to life at the mention of the money, like the *whoomp* of lighter fluid hitting hot coals—and suddenly he understood something: how hunger, essentially a deficit, distilled to its purest form becomes its own opposite, the life force itself. He had seen the same thing in his sister. And maybe that was why Helen ate so much, why Mo stole groceries. Jill seemed to like the feeling, even thrive on it. "You know, when you eat too much, you don't hear so good," she said once. "But when you're smoking rock and you forget to eat, you hear, like, everything on earth, you're like a fucking radar, man."

The supermarket's lot was empty, dotted with scavenging gulls and fallen clots of Spanish moss. "See, they're not even open, it's after ten," he said. "You want me to just drop you off here?"

But she was pointing to the alley. "Around back," she said. "That's where he said to meet him."

He hit the brakes, stopped on an angle under a pole lamp. "Forget it," he said. "I'm not getting in the middle of this, whatever it is. Is your dealer back there or something?"

"Not no *dealer*, I told you," she said. "You can meet him yourself. Or just drop me, if you're such a chicken. Mr. Meek'll take me home." She ran her fingers over the door for the handle. Stoned, she gave off a strange confidence, some chemical imitation of faith.

"All right, then hold on, I'll drive you around back." He didn't know why he was bothering with this last bit of chivalry—as if it would make a difference to her. Maybe habit. Or maybe he just didn't want to feel responsible if something happened to her.

A lone minivan was parked sideways by the row of Dumpsters, its tinted windows flickering under a faulty security light. The man at the van's rear doors was standing so still that Terry, cruising slowly past, almost didn't see him—but then the figure raised an arm, checking his watch.

He had the stout, officious posture, the white shirt and black trousers, of a grocery store manager, but Jill yelled, "That's him!" and scrambled out onto the pavement before Terry could brake.

"Goddammit," he said. He stopped, put the car into park, but she was already up and hobbling around it, palming the hood for balance.

On the ground around the man, Terry saw now, sat the familiar mess of falling-apart shopping bags, Jill's things spilling out of them. Terry leaned to pull shut her door, then got out.

"You Alan's stock boy?" the man called. He held out his hand to Terry, ignoring Jill as he would a pesky dog jumping up and down in his face. "Martin Meek. That man is something, ain't he? You ever see them little bitty amps he makes? Genius." His face was smooth, milky-bland, and agelessly boyish. There was some other quality to it, too, or lack of a quality, something Terry couldn't quite identify. Some kind of well-fed glow, faintly familiar. He couldn't remember the last time he'd seen any face he'd say looked satisfied—maybe that was it.

"You're here to give her a ride home?" he said.

"You kidding me?" Mr. Meek said. He let out a small,

body-shaking laugh. "I'm here as a favor to my buddy Alan. This garbage has been sitting in his garage since he kicked her out—didn't want to hurt her feelings, or something. I said, *Son, the trash man cometh.* She knew the score—I told her I'd be here locking up tonight and if she wasn't here to pick it up it was going into the Dumpster with the wet trash, and that's where it was about to be, if you'd got here two minutes later. I've gotta drive all night tonight."

"Aw, come on, I thought you were here giving away stuff," Jill whined.

"To you? Are you out of your mind?" Mr. Meek said. "You're lucky I don't run you out of town, get the cops on your ass before you suck Alan dry. Man's a goddamn saint, that's his problem. I know your kind. I wouldn't give you a stick of gum. You hear about the giveaways?" he said to Terry.

"Free groceries?" Terry said. "I thought she was lying . . ."

"It's a promotional thing," Mr. Meek said. He ran a hand over his shiny forehead. "You want to get people's attention, help 'em out when you can, but once they get your scent, start acting like animals—then it's time to pack it in and move on. Next stop, where no one knows me from Adam."

"You own grocery stores?" Terry said. He'd known there had to be a logical explanation.

"Buy 'em out, actually," Mr. Meek said. "The giveaways are just a side thing, a charity thing. Like what Alan does." He nodded at Jill, who was gazing at him appreciatively, as if he hadn't just insulted her. "Only I'm not so gullible, I don't let people walk all over me. If they ask me for it, I don't give it to 'em, that's my motto. Boy might be a genius but he's got no common sense. This girl's like the plague, bar your door when you see her coming."

Terry felt uncomfortable, but Jill didn't seem to care. She was busily gathering up her bags, as if this whole transaction were routine. "I thought you told me you were still living with him," he said to her. He would never have given her a ride otherwise, he realized. She was supposed to be Alan's problem. Now she was a hot potato, passed to him.

"Hmm?" she said vaguely, moving things from bag to bag, not looking up.

Terry realized how stupid he sounded, had been.

"Well, all right then," Mr. Meek said, yawning. He patted his trouser pockets, found his keys. "She's not going home with you now, son, is she?"

"No, I just gave her a ride," Terry said. He heard himself, overly indignant, and squared his shoulders, held out his hand to Mr. Meek.

"Good boy. Alan said you were smart." Mr. Meek rolled his eyes at Jill's bent-over back and turned to go. "Take care of yourself."

Terry turned, too—there was nothing else for him to do, no point in trying for a rational conversation with her—and started walking toward his car. There were bus stops, shelters—hell, mini-storage—and a hundred other fools like himself. If anyone could survive, would always survive, it was Jill. Still, he knew if it hadn't been for Mr. Meek, she'd probably be planted in his car right now, or worse, on his couch. He heard the van rev hugely behind him and start to move, brakes tweeting.

He had his car door open, one foot inside, when she hit him, knocked him into the frame, shaking the Honda with her weight, arms and knees and elbows flapping at every part of him like a furious flock of birds. "You owe me!" she was screaming. "You think you could just walk away? You owe me a hundred bucks!"

He fought, trying to pry her off, beat her off, kick her away. Her mass, the force in her wasted body, shocked him. They struggled silently for a moment, the only sound the bug-zapper snap and sizzle of the light over their heads, until finally he got her wrists in a grip. She was leering wildly, almost gleefully, up into his eyes, and he shoved her back away from himself, still holding on to her wrists. "What the hell's wrong with you!" he yelled at her.

"You—owe—me," she panted. "You said, if he was *here* and he *gave* me something."

"Come on, Jill, give me a break. Like I have a hundred bucks. You knew I was just bullshitting."

"Then let me go!"

"I'm not letting go until you fucking settle down."

"I'll be good, I promise!" she cried.

"Fine." He released her. "Why don't you go back to wherever you came from?"

"You owe me a hundred bucks!" she shrieked again. But she stood back out of his range, and she looked strangely unexcited now, like she was only screaming for effect.

"Jill," he said, getting his breath back. "What do you want? You want me to call the cops? I gave you a ride, now leave me the fuck alone."

"Well, give me some money for a cab."

He slid his nylon wallet out of his back pocket. What the hell, he had nothing of value—no credit cards, nothing she could steal. Five bucks, all he had on him, and he'd get off easy. "See?" He pinched out the bill, then opened the billfold like a mouth to show her its black empty inside.

"Okay." She stepped forward suspiciously and took the money. "Hey. Is that him?" She put her hand over his on the wallet, pulled it gently toward her, squinting, then out of his fingers, before he even realized what she was talking about. "He's beautiful," she said.

The picture flashed under the light, between her long thumbs: Chase's small golden face, his shining eyes, spiky hair smoothed by some adult hand into a wave across his forehead. She stood there holding it, no longer angry or threatening. She looked up at Terry quizzically, then back at the photo. "He looks just like you," she said.

The panic hit like a wall of water trying to crash up and out of him, as it always did, as if he could save Chase even now. Jill wasn't going to do anything, she was already holding out the wallet, giving it back. And it was *just a picture,* hadn't he told his sister that a thousand times? *It's not him, it's a picture.* But it was as if the wall had broken something open this time, inside of him or out, he couldn't tell. He heard something that sounded like the earth roaring in his ears, felt it all around him and underneath, the rumble of the great engine grinding them along. He doubled over, queasy, holding his knees.

"Hey, take it easy," Jill was saying. "Don't freak out on me now, man, okay? You'll be okay. You're okay."

She crouched beside him and awkwardly looped her arms around his shoulders, tried to pull his head against her flat chest, her dress's rough smocking creasing into his cheek.

"Aw, you're just a baby," she said. He didn't bother to push her away. When he closed his eyes, he couldn't tell if it was her or the earth rocking him.

Awareness

SILENCE ON THE LINE can have many qualities: the unspoken question mark of confusion; the charged static hum of impatience, perversion, or repressed juvenile hilarity; the unmistakable jagged wordlessness of unrequited love. Operators and receptionists know all these silences by heart—at Cape Fear Memorial we got them all. Only emergency calls were routed automatically through the computerized switchboard, though sometimes there was a system error and we in the Information Hexagon got those, too.

Then, an incident occurred. A lady, one of our patients, went home after surgery and found her own cancerous bladder in her overnight bag. Suddenly my mornings were filled with angry hang ups, cranks, and reporters from tabloid TV shows screaming, "Can you explain how it is possible to lose a bladder!" I never responded, never allowed myself to be provoked, but referred them all to corporate headquarters as we'd been instructed, going ahead and punching them through right then if they wanted, though most of these disconnected, my fault or theirs or the system's I could never tell. The system was so large and complex it had developed a life and intelligence, albeit partial and confused, of its own. It often turned against itself, arbitrarily disconnecting incoming calls, or recording one person's outgoing calls as messages on someone else's voice mail. About once a month men in jumpsuits showed up to service it. "Faulty relay," they might offer, on their way out to their van for a part. "Defective motherboard." Whatever they did never made much difference.

All of us on phones felt bad for the lady who found her bladder. She had seen what she was never supposed to see, and there was no way to take it back. Pulling back the folds of a nightie, something moist against your fingertips. What's this, a Danish, something the kids brought me from the beach? . . . We couldn't stop thinking about it. Her identity was being kept secret, but she had to have walked *right past us* on her way out, happily unaware, that bag slung over her shoulder. Its awful, sodden bundle bouncing invisibly along like a bomb, waiting to ruin her life. Some of us couldn't eat for days.

We talked about chipping in to send her a balloon bouquet, or something from the Notions Kiosk, but Administration got wind of our plan and asked if we were insane. Liability, hello!, they shouted at us. Think about it, use your imaginations, the PR bitch—everyone called her that behind her back—scolded us at a special meeting with sprinkle cookies and punch, as if we were learning-disabled kindergartners. Would you like to open any more packages from the hospital if you were that lady? she asked us.

We *were* using our imaginations. But fine, we sent nothing, though there remained some bad feeling on our part because we, not PR, were the ones on the front lines, fending off the calls, which continued for weeks after the incident, after the orderly responsible for the mistake had been fired, the case turned over to attorneys for settlement.

Then, just as the complaints started letting up and things started settling down, Lawanda on the late shift began getting bomb threats. "Probably that bladder lady's family," she said, "and I don't blame 'em." Security didn't believe her, though—none of us did at first. The overnight workers were, as a rule, either constitutionally unflappable or else loons, no middle ground, and Lawanda was spooky. She grimaced and rolled her eyes randomly when she spoke, implying a world of ineffable threat and significant invisible current only she could perceive, and she always carried a tire iron, as an apparent weapon against the intangible. She seemed more bothered by the bladder than anybody, but about the threats she was maddeningly vague, never reporting them when they happened but waiting, terrifyingly, until the next day, or even a few days later. And she refused to repeat what the caller had actually said. "It's not what they said, but what they were fixing to say," she told Security when they pressed her for specifics, or just: "It wasn't like that."

Security finally gave up, told her to let them know when she had something more solid. False bomb threats were a felony, they warned us all in a memo, and would be *prosecuted to the fullest extent of the law.* "Who they think they talking to?" Lawanda demanded, twitching away, to anyone who would listen. In the meantime, we were to follow procedure, the memo said. Even I knew this was an insult.

Procedure was a form, gummed pads of which were kept by every telephone extension in the building, called the "Bomb Threat Checklist." It resembled a regular phone message slip but with quadruple the options crammed into its three-by-five space, and it appeared to have been authored in around 1961, or ordered from the back of a comic book. *In the event of a threatening call,* it instructed, *do not interrupt caller except to ask: 1. When will it go off? 2. Where is it planted? 3. What does it look like? 4. Why are you doing this? 5. Who are you?* The bottom was filled with check-off boxes, with a note to *please check all that apply. Background noises: office machines, factory machines, street traffic, airplanes, trains, animals, music, party atmosphere, bedlam, other. Speech characteristics: fast, slow, juvenile, nasal, stutter, slurred, raspy, intoxicated, pleasant, sotto voce, other.* It went on and on. *Bedlam?* Did anyone in the nineties know what that was? I'd never seen anyone use the Bomb Threat Checklist or even acknowledge its existence, except new employees on their first day, asking if it was for real.

"I thought the system had a call-trace thing built into it," I said to Lawanda. "Didn't they show us that during training?"

"Yeah, but it don't work for cell phones," she said. "Ain't nothing they can do." She looked darkly satisfied.

I pictured myself sitting obediently in my ergonomic chair trying to check off the appropriate boxes as bricks and cement rained down. Security were assholes. Yes, Lawanda was crazy, but I believed her that someone was calling, *something* was happening. I could tell when I had complainers on the line before they even spoke, so I could imagine how the silence surrounding a bomb threat would crackle, making words irrelevant. We'd all seen the footage, people in new cities each week running from public buildings with charred faces, the mug shots of disgruntled, mustachioed loners—why wasn't Security more concerned?

The other operators didn't seem worried either—they laughed at Lawanda, whirled their index fingers beside their ears at the mention of her name—but I felt a new loyalty toward her. We only ever saw each other for moments, on days when our shifts overlapped, yet I found her familiar and friendly as a planet, arriving at the same time each night, aglow with unknowable energy, departing palely at dawn. Plus, she and I made up an odd group of two, years younger or older than the others, no cowboy husbands picking us up in outrageously detailed trucks, no tacked-up photos of grandbabies. We possessed equally dubious diplomas, which we had compared during our training session: mine from the local business college, hers from the Sunshine Recovery House. I stopped her as she was leaving one morning and told her I believed her and would do whatever I could to help, would let her know first thing if I got any suspicious calls.

"Oh, you'll get the call," she said. "Only a matter of time." She shuddered. "Ever wonder what the Devil sounds like? You take a piece of him, he wants a piece of you."

"So it was a man who called?" I said. She hadn't even told Security that much.

"It wasn't no man," she said. "But thanks, baby, I knew you believed me. You'll back me up, right?"

"Of course," I said.

"I mean, why would I want to make them threats myself," she said.

"Right," I said.

"I mean, I been to see her and everything. I had to see her face to face, hear her side of the story."

"What?" I said.

She stepped closer, put her red-penciled mouth next to my ear. "I'm telling you, she will never be the same," she said.

"Who!" I said, though I knew who she meant. "When did you see her? She *told* you she was making the threats?" The whole thing was absurd—why would the woman admit to it, and jeopardize the millions she was about to win? Plus, there was no way to access a patient address or medical file without authorization, which I knew Lawanda could never get.

"Her hair had a white stripe this thick," Lawanda said. She measured an inch with her fingers, and held them up against her hairline. "Right here. Turned white the day she found that bladder." Lots of patients had that stripe when they checked out, I knew; it was just their dye jobs growing out. But that didn't mean Lawanda was lying about seeing the woman. "She will never be the same," she repeated, with convincing reverence. "Never the same."

"Okay, you better tell me what's going on," I began. "First of all, when did you see her? How did you find out where she lives?"

"Oh, that ain't hard. She lives way out, off Route 111. Big ol' house, one of them Cape Cods. She don't need the money, I'm telling you that much, that ain't why she's suing. You know what I saw in her yard? I'm not making this up. A calf walking backwards. Just like it says in the Bible. A little baby calf, walking a straight line over to its mama, but *backwards.*"

"The Bible?" I said. "Where does it say—"

"Shh!" Lawanda hissed. A pair of nursing supervisors came around the corner and moved toward us, importantly discussing a file one of them was holding, pointedly not saying hello to us.

Lawanda focused fiercely on me, the way you never do with coworkers, and I noticed things I never had before about her face: a milky housecat skittishness in her eyes, odd, deep creases around her mouth that were neither frown nor smile lines. "How's it going with you and Kenny Pham?" she asked in a bright loud voice not quite her own.

"Not so good," I said.

She nodded and her gaze retracted a bit, drew itself in politely. "He's cute," she said, "but he ain't getting none of *my* blood." She covered her gold-festooned neck with both hands, protecting it from Dracula, then suddenly laughed for no reason, whirled, and darted off to the glass-doored exit to catch the transit bus pulling up into a patch of sun outside. The nursing supervisors watched her go.

The system buzzed then, as if on cue, and I grabbed my headset, heart pounding, but it was only a woman, weeping, wanting to know what room her father was in. Disappointed, I helped her. I had no idea what I'd have said if it had been Lawanda's caller, but I suddenly felt the terrorist's presence more strongly than ever, as if he—or she— were hiding somewhere nearby, waiting and watching my every move.

She's lying, crazy, I told myself. I was crazy to listen to her, we could both get fired. Yet I felt weirdly exhilarated. I caught myself hoping—foolishly, like a child hopes for a hurricane—that she was telling the truth. About everything: the calls, the lady, the calf, everything.

I WAS DYING to tell somebody, but no way could I tell Kenny Pham. He didn't believe in the threats to begin with, and he certainly had no special concern for my safety. "Ha ha, Lawanda," he'd said when I first told him about the investigation—word of it hadn't reached Pathology, where he worked—"Ha ha, oh, that Lawanda," as though amused by the antics of a little dog.

"What do you mean, 'Ha ha, Lawanda'?"

"Oh, you know," he said. "Lawanda. No one takes her seriously. Besides, if Security was really worried, they'd evacuate us, or at least let us know they were investigating—

I mean, we're the ones with the patients' lives in our hands. Okay, listen." He went back to reading me the vows he was helping write for his twin brother's gay wedding. " 'George, I give myself to you without reserve . . . ' "

He made having a gay twin brother seem like something he'd generously thought up himself, in the same way that some white people bragged about adopting black or drug-addicted babies. We were supposed to be on a date, I'd thought, but he had on scrubs for one of the extra, volunteer shifts he put in to head Cape Fear's blood donation drive. His med-tech ID photo beamed out from his breastbone, a miniature version of his beseeching cherubic face— two of him trying to get people's blood at once, impossible to resist. He was ten years my junior, cloyingly boyish with almost zero body hair except on the lower half of his legs, as though the hair were caught there in its attempt to migrate off his body and find a more hospitable host, one less likely to harvest it and give it away. Who could blame it? I pictured the hair catching a ride with me in a convertible I didn't own, Thelma and Louise, making for the hills.

I couldn't kayak or cave-dive or rappel, any of the things Kenny loved, and I was no longer eligible to give blood because of an immune disorder, discovered a few months ago

during my annual check-up, around the same time, mysteriously, that he and I started dating. My blood had lost its
ability to distinguish between "self" and "other," the hematologist told me, and so was dutifully destroying its own
cells, ruining my capacity to clot. My antibodies were like
out-of-control guard dogs, he said, and my spleen, which he
was considering removing, was like a crack house—"not
the source of the problem, but where the problem congre-
gates and conducts its activities." "Picture your immune system as an engine kicked into overdrive," he said. I liked this
hematologist, he resembled Tim Conway, but his endless
metaphors gave me nightmares.

Diagnosis had taken forever—weeks—during which
time he encouraged me to become familiar with the
"possible scenarios." I had a marrow biopsy, a needle
pushed into my hipbone. I had death dreams: the packing-
for-a-long-trip dream, the being-led-by-masked-doctors-
through-progressively-smaller-rooms dream, the dream of
the partially invisible polar bears. That last one, actually,
had probably come from something I'd seen on TV, but
that didn't diminish its scariness. Sometimes Kenny Pham
was one of the masked dream doctors, leading me down the
narrowing, darkening corridors, and I would plead with

him breathlessly to stop, listen to me, tell me what was going on. He would pause, pull down his mask and smile gently but say nothing, his eyes fixed in their attitude of robotic compassion.

In real life, we said, *How ironic, how paradoxical.* He collected blood, and I could not stop bleeding. What a coincidence. This sounded like a lie to me, but I couldn't think what the truth might be. The logic of why he might be attracted to me, or I to him, when neither of us could give the other what we most wanted—he, my blood, and I, his sympathy.

As it turned out, my disease was chronic, the hematologist finally pronounced, but not progressive. I could keep my spleen, would not require treatment, only "monitoring," and would likely live another fifty years—as long as I quit the rugby team, he deadpanned, Conway-like. Sometimes blood trickled out of my nose without warning, and I bruised easily and dramatically, like bad fruit, from the slightest poke, or from leaning against a hard surface. But I wasn't going to die.

Actually, though, dying wasn't my biggest fear. Worse than dying was something I read about in a magazine in the hematologist's waiting room, a medical phenomenon

referred to as "intraoperative awareness": when a surgery
patient who appeared to be under successful general anes-
thesia in fact remained conscious throughout the entire operation, awake but immobilized, unable to communicate
that he could feel and see and hear everything that was happening. Apparently this occurred frequently, countless times
a year, but was little recognized, underreported, since doctors tended not to believe patients who said they had experienced it. Only when the patient repeated some irrelevant
detail he could not have known, from when he was supposed to be asleep, like what the nurse said she'd had for
lunch or the knock-knock joke the surgeon told, did the
doctors finally acknowledge it could be true. But even then
it was hard to sue, there being no reliable, scientific measure
of pain or fear.

Though the story about this was in his own magazine,
my hematologist claimed never to have heard of intraoperative awareness, but said I shouldn't worry, if I ended up
needing surgery all our anesthesiologists were kick-ass
—that was what he said, "kick-ass." Still, the image
haunted me: lying there, mind awake but muscles frozen,
voice trapped in my throat as if by voodoo, the doctors'
faces moving in and out of view under a pockmarked

acoustic-tile ceiling, large hands moving around like blood-soaked moles inside me. My self opened up like a dumb machine, saturated with awareness I didn't want.

I had never been superstitious, but now, newly fragile, I wondered about altered states, the nature of consciousness. I tore up the organ-and-tissue donor card Kenny had brought me to sign, told him I'd changed my mind.

"But your organs are uncompromised," he protested. "And besides, I thought you of all people understood the need. You might have needed marrow, you know, if your diagnosis had gone the other way."

"Maybe organs aren't meant to be perpetual-motion machines," I said. I was remembering the stories I'd heard of transplant recipients waking up from their surgeries with sudden, uncharacteristic cravings, yearnings for Michelob or chicken fingers or a ride on a Harley, affinities that had somehow lived on in the cells of the dead person's heart, or liver, or pancreas—how traumatized and exhausted those poor organs must be, expecting some decent rest and then, at the last moment, thanks to technology, put back to work for another fifty years. I was thinking of the little boy from Seattle who'd been identified as the reincarnation of a famous Buddhist monk and whisked off to Nepal, his first

words when he got off the plane, to the crowd of monks
awaiting their leader's return: *It was a long way, and I was
tired of walking....* And I was remembering something that
had happened when I was a small child, three or four: I'd
gotten stuck riding a tricycle that ran on a wooden figure-
eight track, at some carnival, and believed I had to keep
steering, keep pedaling, until the track came to an end, only
it just kept going around and around, until I was sobbing,
Let me off, I can't make it stop, I can't make it stop!

"Organs don't have memories, that's just a myth," Kenny
said. "Or power of suggestion. There's no scientific evidence
to support that."

"People saying how they feel," I said. "That's evidence."

"I thought you knew better than to believe that BS," he
said. Of course Kenny never swore. "You know, your body
alone could save fifty lives."

"My life," I said. "I want it to save my life. I'm sorry if
that's selfish but it is my body, isn't it?"

"Of course," he said reasonably. But in his tawny eyes I
saw something else—a darkening I had earlier mistaken for
love, when he'd accompanied me to the lab for blood work,
or phoned to get my biopsy results early, or murmured,
We'd better not, I don't want to bruise you. Now I recog-

nized the look for what it was: pity, tinged with moral disdain. He was disappointed in me. I was living, yes, but not living up to his standards. Doctors always loved the brave, and I wasn't. He himself gave a pint each month, as frequently as was allowed, showily toting along a copy of *Mother Jones* or the *Utne Reader* to demonstrate how routine this was for him, how selflessly and sensibly he made use of the twenty minutes it took to drain the blood from his body. *George, I give myself to you without reserve.*

Why had I ever found virtue attractive? I wondered. Why did he have to care about everyone, why couldn't he just care about me?

"You know, I see people sicker than you every day," he said. "My mother said her breast cancer actually increased her awareness of other people's suffering. She signed up to be a donor while she was still having chemo."

"Yeah, well, I don't have a mother," I said. It wasn't technically true, but close enough. My mother's idea of a funny anecdote was to tell about the time when I was five and she spanked me so hard her hand ached and then I turned around and said, *That didn't hurt.* I suspected her, in fact, to be the source of my disease—if it was true that one internalized the voices and wishes of one's parents. Despite her best efforts she had been unable to obliterate me, so now my body had to do it itself.

Kenny looked pious, as though he'd caught me in a lie. "You showed me a photo of your mother," he said. "Standing with a snow shovel, in front of a house." As though the shovel and the house made her real.

Sometimes, pushed to the wall, I'd ask, *Who do you think you are, Jesus Christ?*

Card-carrying secular humanist that he was, he only laughed at that.

The real question was why I didn't just dump him. When I was healthy, love and nothing less could undo me. My solitude had seemed pleasant and faintly honorable, something that might pass for integrity. I paid my own rent and slept soundly, secure in my ability to let go of losers. But now there was a flaw in the works, the machinery of my self no longer trustworthy. My own blood was betraying me; what could a boyfriend possibly do that was worse? I flailed, like any animal, grasping for the nearest life form and hanging on, trying to pull myself back into life as I'd known it, the way you had to live it if you didn't want to go around flinching and muttering and carrying a tire iron: unconscious, uncompromised, willfully impervious to threat.

"It's ridiculous to worry about a bomb," Kenny said, standing in his doorway and motioning for me to hurry so he could lock up behind me. "More people will die today from lack of blood than from any bomb, believe me."

I misheard him, then realized of course I was wrong. For a moment, I'd thought he said: *More people will die today from lack of love . . .*

I IMAGINED WHAT would happen to Lawanda if I reported her, the downward slide back into the loop of jail and halfway houses, the shape of her life like the closing-in corridors of my nightmares—my fault, for bearing the guilty knowledge. I couldn't tell what part of her story was truth, but I half-wished the hospital would blow, just to teach everyone a lesson.

But of course the wrong people would get hurt, or killed. The patients, hundreds of them, men and women and children and babies, humble in their ugly gowns, all of them wishing they'd never met us, learning more than they'd ever wanted to know about their bodies' private business, not necessarily brave, or sober, or sane, but still, most of the time, saying *Please* and *Thank you* to everyone and meaning it.

I thought about it overnight, gave that one night to fate. I wouldn't tell Security or Kenny, I finally decided, wouldn't give them the satisfaction, but would grab one of the administrative higher-ups when they came by the Hexagon as they did on the way to their offices each morning, showing off to one another that they knew us, the hired help, by name, used the same entrance we did. I would mention what she'd said offhandedly, as if I didn't realize the implications, and it would come back to her vaguely, anonymously, her punishment perhaps getting watered down in the process.

I didn't sleep, my mind spinning out images of demolition, girders poking bonelike out of concrete, uniformed men carrying children through flames—and always, that bladder, black and damaged and glistening, the source of so much ruin, obscene as a secret exposed.

In the morning I felt weighted down with a wooziness I recognized as signifying a drop in my platelet count—I'd get Kenny to take a sample on my lunch break. It was raining leadenly, windlessly, and driving through it I felt my blood pound in response, as if it longed to burst past the pointless boundary of my body and assimilate, equalize the universe at last.

The building was still standing, but it looked frail in a new way, its beams and bones palpably *there,* just beneath its pink-bricked surface. The blue lights of a sheriff's cruiser were flashing in the turnaround where the transit buses ran, and I could see too many people standing in the lobby— staff in their various-colored scrubs, operators I didn't think were on duty, damp onlookers who'd stepped in from outside, and even a few paper-robed, worried-looking patients. The men in jumpsuits were there, too, I saw, clustered around a giant tangle of wires they had pulled out from a wall box. One of them recognized me and put a hand on my arm as I pushed my way through. "You notice a lot of hang-ups lately?" he said.

"Just the usual," I said. A few every day, wrong numbers or mistakes from some telemarketer, already disconnected by the time I got on the line—a blank, automated silence that had no qualities at all. These couldn't be the calls Lawanda had meant.

"Well, we finally got it," the man said. "We thought we had it before, but now we've really got it. You won't be getting no more of them hang-ups."

"What was it?" I asked. "What's going on?"

"Oh, they're gonna tell you all about it at the meeting."

"What meeting?"

"Idiots," Lawanda hissed, behind me. "It wasn't the system, it was that *lady.*" I thought she was talking to us, but when I turned I saw she was several yards away, the crowd clearing space for her as she shouted into the face of a sheriff's deputy, who had her tire iron, I saw, sticking out of his armpit like a broken limb. He was banding her wrists together with a plastic tie. Her eyes scanned over me, wild with light, but she didn't see me. "Wasn't no *harassment* about it!" she yelled, but everyone was already ignoring her, the cuffed criminal, the lunatic being led safely away.

A cadre of nurses began hustling the onlookers back to wherever they'd come from with that "Okay, show's over" briskness. The PR bitch clicked around in her heels, grinning at everyone and handing out yellow sheets of paper —a memo, I saw when I got mine, announcing an "informational meeting" for all phone staff in ten minutes. "What's going on, what happened?" I asked her, my voice false.

"Don't worry, everything's fine," she said.

"I know," I snapped. "Can you just tell me what's going on?"

"Relax," she said. Her face, which I had never seen up

close, was as small-featured and blandly empathetic as an anchorwoman's, or a Beanie Baby's. Kenny suddenly popped up next to her, his elbow touching hers, I noticed. They had matching teardrop-shaped I GAVE stickers stuck on their chests. His tanned, scrubbed face was handsome as ever, aglow with health and goodwill.

"Sorry about your friend," he said.

"What did she do?" I said. "I mean, I'm sure she didn't do anything."

"Well, it's confidential, really, but I can see you're very concerned," the PR bitch said. She cut her eyes at Kenny, doing this for his approval, I could tell. He nodded at her, encouraging. "She broke the patient-confidentiality rule. And the Sheriff's Department wants to question her about the bomb threats she reported."

"I'm sure she didn't make those threats," I said.

"Oh, we know that," the PR bitch said. "But she did contact a patient during her off hours, and that is a violation."

"Did the patient complain?" I said.

"Well, that's not really the point," she said.

"But what if she was friends with the patient?" I said. "Or if she was helping the patient in some way, or checking on her to make sure she was okay—"

"That's just not the case here, unfortunately," the PR bitch said. "It was the patient's attorney who brought it to our attention. So it doesn't matter if they were best friends, it's still a potential liability."

"That makes a lot of sense," Kenny said.

"What?" I said.

"I'm just saying I understand the hospital's position," he said.

"You know what? I'm going to leave the two of you alone," the PR bitch said.

"You're an asshole," I said to Kenny.

He seemed mildly surprised, not offended. "I'm sorry you feel that way," he said. "Can we discuss this rationally at some point?"

"No," I said.

The PR bitch, who hadn't moved, looked horrified—more so, I thought, than our words warranted. Her eyes were wide and fixed on my arm, her mouth curled in dainty disgust. I bent my head and looked where she was looking, at a large, dark splat of blood, which had apparently just landed, locustlike and out of nowhere, on my wrist. Several more drops kamikazed down, then, from my nose, spotting the white tile between my feet. I stared at them, mesmerized as always by their scary beauty, their promise of a story I could never fully know.

"Don't worry," I heard Kenny tell her reassuringly. "It's nothing."

"THE PURPOSE OF this meeting is to let you know we have completed a thorough investigation and determined there is no legitimate threat of any bomb situation at the present time," the security chief said. He was a balding, muscle-bound man who I knew Lawanda hated personally —"that pumped-up narc," she called him. I'd tried, before the meeting started, to talk to him, persuade him she hadn't done anything wrong, could not have made the threats, but he'd just raised his eyebrows at me. "We already know that," he said. "We had a trace on the system for sixty days, trying to catch that guy who got fired, you know, for putting that bladder in that lady's suitcase. Turns out it wasn't him either. But that's how we got her on the false threats, 'cause we checked every call that came in, and none of them was any kind of threat."

He read, now, with as little expression as possible, from a clipboard. "In the course of our investigation, we did discover a telecommunications system error which some of you may have experienced over the past month or so, but which has now been identified and corrected. In short, due to a programming error, the system was placing calls to itself. It was supposed to be programmed to call the telecommunications office when it was due for its scheduled maintenance, but the hospital's main number was accidentally programmed in instead. When one of you answered, it would disconnect, but not immediately, so that was the silence you experienced. At any rate, there should be no more problems, and, as usual, ha ha, it was the humans' fault, not the computer's." Everyone laughed, automatically and dutifully, like a sitcom audience, and some of them held up their hands to ask questions.

I stopped listening then. I clutched a Kleenex wad to my face, feeling a kind of terrible hope. Kenny and I would no longer speak, I was sure, and he would look at me with open pity whenever we crossed paths. But a system error— that was something that could easily happen again, would almost certainly happen, only a matter of time. Lawanda might be back by then, or she might never be allowed to return. But sooner or later, the system would accomplish what she and I and all the frustrated callers we'd ever listened to, all confounded and compromised by our humanity, never could.

I pictured its dark innards, the unnamed spaces between tiny, magnetic components—and somewhere in there, a programmed longing that could never be fulfilled, a voice no one could hear, calling, *Hello? Hello? Why aren't you answering?* And: *If you weren't going to answer, why did you make me this way, why did you program me to call?* It would try over and over, for months, just to reach somebody, to make itself understood. And then, in despair or just plain weary, it would prepare to blow itself to pieces, taking with it all who had refused to believe.

REMNANTS OF EARL

I WAS TRYING to describe this man I would probably never see again, but it was harder than I thought. "If you could see him, you would understand everything," I told Eddie on the phone. "Big shoulders, but not fake big—real big, comfortably big, like a sofa. Like he was just made that way. White-blond hair, like your rabbit, thin hair but not thin*ing*, you know what I mean? It's baby-fine, that's what it is—and actually, he kind of looks like a baby! Kind of like the Gerber baby, only if the Gerber baby were angry, and rode a motorcycle. You know what I mean? I mean, *he* doesn't ride a motorcycle, he just *looks* like a guy who rides a motorcycle. Or maybe not quite that angry—more like the quiet younger brother of a guy who rides a motorcycle. He's like, the brother who doesn't have anything to prove. Like there are motorcycles in the family, he's comfortable around motorcycles, but he himself can take or leave motorcycles."

"I can totally picture him," Eddie said. Our TVs were tuned to the same channel, producing that weird unison echo effect where you can't tell which end the music and voices are coming from. From both ends also came the on-off rush of rain from the remnants of Earl, which had done some damage to the Panhandle but weakened before reaching us. Something about our location in the middle of the peninsula, sunk in a prehistoric basin, made storms bypass us. We got feeder bands, spun-off twisters, remnants and remains, but never the real thing.

"And even though he has that baby hair and face," I continued, "he gives off a kind of *man* feeling. He's not boyish. I hate boyish."

"I know you do," Eddie said. "Remember Post-it?"

A couple years ago I'd dated a boyish lifeguard named Memo, who referred to his own hair unironically as his "mop of curls" and literally panted with eagerness, even when we were just sitting around watching reruns. Everyone loved him for this quality but I thought it was a stupid quality. He made me feel stodgy, cranky, anything but girlish —he made me feel like Andy Rooney.

Eddie had helped me extricate myself from that and many subsequent relationships by teaching me tricks such as deliberately putting on and lacing up my shoes when an unwanted guest stopped by, or hanging up on myself mid-sentence when someone called. Our friendship, in fact, had consisted largely of helping each other get into and out of relationships. But as my relationships became progressively more imaginary, Eddie's had grown increasingly, alarmingly real. This seemed to suggest something about our respective goals that I didn't feel like thinking about.

"This guy's nothing like Memo," I told him. "He's a young man, yes, but he knows whatever it is old men know. I have no idea what I mean by that. But it's true." I pictured the guy's mildly fierce, slightly abashed face, so alive you could see knowledge and recognition and sneaky thoughts flowing in and out of it, despite the unsuccessful way he tried to hide this, his squinting, sidelong way of looking at people, eyes narrowed as if by decades of light and beauty and pain. Only he hadn't been alive decades. Two and a half, I guessed. "If you could see him, you would under-stand everything," I said.

"He sounds exactly like this guy I dated in Mobile," Eddie said. "The question is, what are you going to do?"

"God, get off my case," I said.

"Well, what's his name?" Eddie said.

"I don't know," I muttered. "He's the air-conditioning guy, I told you."

"Well, Jesus," Eddie said. "You could at least—what? Hold on." I heard a new voice, male, intimate and distinct, only on his end, not on mine.

"Is that him, your new friend?" I said. For some reason Eddie was being secretive about his latest, a stylist who cut hair with him at Fantastic Sam's and lip-synched on week-ends under the stage name Mary K. Cosmetic. I was dying to meet him, but somehow it was never the right time. They always wanted to be alone, and Eddie refused, supersti-tiously, to tell me the guy's real name; the moment he ut-tered it, he said, they'd break up. "Why didn't you tell me you had company?" I said.

"Nothing," Eddie said nonsensically. "Oh, something's beeping. Gotta go." He clicked off. Nothing had been beeping.

"Fine," I said to my kitchen, "be that way." Some drops

popped noncommittally on the crank-slat window. I had been saving the news that I'd gotten fired again to tell Eddie in person, when he came over to sit out the non-storm like we always did, breaking out the candles at the first flicker of the lights and gorging on Slim Jims and Bloody Marys, Eddie entertaining me with whatever tricks he was practicing, his floating zombie ball or Chinese linking rings, refusing to say how they worked no matter how drunk I got him. But now it looked like he wasn't coming.

MANPOWER, WHERE I TEMPED, had AC problems. Lightning struck the outside fan the day I started—a miracle, I thought, but later I learned it got hit every couple weeks. The condenser went out one month, the compressor the next. Wiring got chewed through by squirrels. Nondairy creamer from the coffee cart got sucked into the intake and contaminated the ducts, coloring the office air hazy white with spores. Every week, one at at a time, a different part of the system died and had to be replaced, reminding me of a philosophy problem, or maybe a Zen koan, I'd heard somewhere: If the blade of your favorite knife wears down and you replace it, and then the handle breaks so you replace that, is it still the same knife—your favorite?

The repair guy worked more hours than we did, everyone joked, yet nobody knew his name. The breast patch on his shirt said GEOFF, but I overheard Mr. Giancursio call him that once and he'd said, "Oh no, Geoff's my buddy." Another time he used my desk phone to call in to headquarters, and when they answered he said, "Hey, this is Corey," but then a second later he burst out laughing at the person on the other end and yelled, "Gotcha, didn't I?"

The problem with finding out someone's name was that the more you wanted to know it, the more impossible it became to casually ask. Because I cared so much, I couldn't ask him, or anybody, outright; it would have been impossible to keep the desperate edge out of my voice. Instead, I waited for someone to say it.

I had been waiting about six months when I got fired. I was only a temp, hired to help hire other temps, but still, it was a shock. "You've broken the dress code for the last time," Mr. Giancursio told me in his glass-walled office. He sounded jubilant, even congratulatory, but he was gazing at my armpits with genuine, personal distaste—disgusted not only as a professional, but as a man.

"But the AC's down, it's like a hundred in here, everyone

is sleeveless," I said. It was true. Out in the computer room the data girls, college kids on summer break, tapped away at their keyboards, their freckled shoulders prettily reflecting the fluorescent overheads. I couldn't believe he'd discriminate so obviously.

"They've got jackets," he said.

"My jacket's right over there," I said, inclining my head violently in the direction of my cubicle—too self-conscious now to raise my arm and point.

"Look, I warned you when we hired you your days were numbered," Mr. Giancursio said. "The girls are here on internships, and you're just . . ." He patted his comb-over and regarded a crumbling ceiling tile, then his staple remover, then a stain on his chair arm. Behind his head in the window the first wisps of Earl floated ominously by, like the ghosts of his lost hair, longing to return.

"What am I?" I said.

"What?"

"You were just going to say what I was."

"What? What are you talking about? Look, you're a smart lady. You're overqualified—you should be more ambitious. Get out of this college town."

"Wait a minute," I said. "I'm a 'lady' and they're 'girls'? Hello, have you ever heard of ageism?"

"Ho *ho*!" Mr. Giancursio said, like some psychotic Santa, his eyebrows shooting up. "Okay, you want to know what this is about? I was trying to give you a break, but I'll tell you what this is about. Try: total disregard for Manpower policy. Try: leaving five to seven minutes early every single day. Try: drinking other people's Slim-Fasts—not that it's helping any. Try: spending all your time bothering the repair guy."

"Did he complain?" I asked, my stomach and palms going cold.

"You think I don't know you've temped for every agency in town? You think we don't talk to each other? You're lucky nobody's suing you for breach of contract. You play games like that, you get a reputation. You college *graduates,* I swear, are worse than the student interns—at least they're responsible, and *grateful.* And I'll tell you what else, I've got a list of ladies this long, moms with kids to feed, who would kill for your position. You've had every advantage, so why should I take pity on you? Why not help people who appreciate it? Your problem, my friend, plain and simple, is *attitude.*"

"Did the repair guy say something?" I said.

"Oh, for God's sake. Work the rest of the day if you want," Mr. Giancursio said, "but then that's it. You've had your chance."

Packing up my few belongings and some office supplies I thought might come in handy someday, I tried not to think of the repair guy. I thought about Eddie's and my ongoing debate, ever since we'd both turned thirty-five the same month, about whether it was all over for us—whether it was still worth trying to find the perfect job, the perfect man, lose twenty pounds, or whether we should just give up, surrender to the speeded-up downhill roll of time. There were two schools of thought on this question, the talk-show school of thought, which said it was never too late to change your life, thirty was the new twenty, whatever age Oprah was at the moment was the age of enlightenment. The other school of thought was reality: It was all over for us.

Eddie was better than I at sustaining the Oprah school of thought, not that he respected Oprah personally ("Has anyone noticed she now thinks she's God?" he often asked, rhetorically). He was saving his tip money toward a move to Vegas, the only place people really paid to see magic, he

212 ► WENDY BRENNER

said, and meanwhile he tirelessly took gigs at local pubs, going from table to table in his ruffled shirtfront doing coin
and card tricks, ignoring drunk frat boys calling him "fag-
got" to his face. Before Mary K. Cosmetic, he'd dated a series of awful locals, rednecks and speed freaks, shifty guys
he knew from beauty school or the magic store. He sometimes phoned me at three A.M. after a nightmare date to
complain, but instead of telling me what went wrong—I'd
have to drag that out of him weeks later—he'd end up ex-
plaining some magic-related concept he'd finally mastered:
You must become the rabbit, he'd say, or *Levitation is all
in the hips.* When I went to see him perform, I felt embarrassed for him, then ashamed of myself. He knew something I didn't, I thought. On both fronts, magic and men, he
never seemed to give up hope.

On the other hand, I didn't think I had either. I couldn't
pinpoint the moment I'd gone from dating men to thinking
about dating them. It wasn't a decision, but more like a
gradual sliding away, a natural receding from gross reality,
like the tide going out. I'd given plenty of guys a chance,
kept an open mind—no one could accuse me of setting my
standards too high. I'd gone along with everything. With

Memo. With my college boyfriend, Moses, who made me
have a threesome with his old Boy Scout buddy, the two of
them giggling whenever their hands accidentally touched on
my body and joking, "Good friends are hard to come by!"
"What are you complaining about," Moses said. "You're
big enough to take on two." I'd modeled nude for Shawn,
a woodcut artist, who told me after a few months of dating that his previous girlfriend had "real hair, not like
yours." Hair he could carve. And then there was Bruce, the
bouncer at Club Neoplasm, who would let me in free to All-
U-Can-Drink Night if I let him stick his hand down my shirt
in front of the crowd. Then he'd make the same offer to all
the girls behind me in line, and I'd rush in to the bar so I
didn't have to watch. All in all, as far as I was concerned, I'd
done my time in the real world. No one could say I hadn't
tried.

It was hard to say when, exactly, my faith began to fal-
ter, after which one of these experiences did I start packing
it in. In my mind, I still believed in the perfect man. That
was the place for him—in my mind. Keeping him there
seemed a good way to keep him alive, and safe, just as my
temp jobs were, I thought, a good way to keep my options

214 • W E N D Y   B R E N N E R

open, keep from getting stuck. If I didn't have a single burning ambition, like Eddie, at least I wouldn't get bogged down in the wrong job, the wrong relationship. I'd float along, free and unfettered, and simply wait for my destiny to arrive—I'd know it when I saw it, or him. Eddie didn't agree with my strategy, but that was okay. Everyone had to find their own way, wasn't that Oprah's big point, more or less?

I took the long way around the back of the building to the parking lot so as not to have to walk by the wall of windows, on view for everyone, the bad example going home. The light was strange, the sky shaded yet overbright like during an eclipse, everything painfully outlined. Slow, frond-shaped shadows moved across the office's stucco façade, their source mysterious—nothing grew near the building. When I moved past I cast no shadow. And there was no place to hide or get discreetly by the repair guy, set up right in my path, crouched on his heels observing the silent AC box as if it were a terrarium or a TV. His hair blazed in the weird light, bringing tears to my eyes. *All illusions are derived from five basic ideas,* I remembered Eddie telling me—*appearance, disappearance, transformation, levitation, and sawing.*

He was humming, I heard as I got close, and then he sang a line, *You can't take that away from me,* a calm grandfatherly lilt to his voice. How did a young man know such an old song? And how did he know to sing it now, so casually, as my excuse for a life collapsed around me, again, like a card trick I hadn't practiced enough?

"I just got freon-certified," he said, when he saw me standing behind him.

"That's great, congratulations," I said.

"No, the point is, I shouldn't have been here all this time until now," he said. He gave a small, amazed laugh. "I was an impostor."

"Well, your secret's safe with me," I said. "I just got fired."

"You're kidding me." His surprise seemed genuine; his face was open and wry and curious, the opposite of impostor. He stood and shook out his shoulders in a series of shrugs and readjustments, like shaking a vest or harness into place. It was a thoughtless, beautiful gesture, something a horse or service dog would do.

"No big deal," I said.

"That sucks," he said. "Why don't you let me buy you a drink? I mean make you one. I bartend weeknights, at— what's your favorite drink?"

"How old are you?" I said.

"Probably your age," he said, suddenly looking hopeful and impulsive, like a gambler. "We were probably in high school at the same time."

Maybe it could work, I thought, maybe younger men were the answer. Yes, I was fat, but my skin was smooth, and I still got carded sometimes at the liquor store, though the clerk may simply have believed I was an undercover cop, misunderstanding my tight, suspicious expression. Still, I'd always loved blond men, because they seemed so foreign, an exotic antidote to my own darkness. When I was little I'd play a game with my baby-sitter: "Pretend I'm a blond girl," I'd say. "Okay," she'd say. That was the whole game—I couldn't imagine any further.

I studied his face, trying to be a gambler myself, trying not to feel like an impostor, trying to believe it was still possible for something good to happen to me. It wasn't a problem of knowing what I wanted, it was a question of whether there was anything left of me to receive it, should it finally arrive.

"The Mafia Café," he said. "You know where that is, right? I just started, but I'm learning to make a pretty mean martini." The box whirred into life beside him, then, and he turned back to it in delight. "What do you know?" he said. "Miracles happen."

I edged away, wishing I could just vanish before anything changed, before the machinery broke down again, before the anomalous light faded and Earl blew over and everything went back to its normal, ugly self. "Hey!" I heard him call, when I had almost made it to my car. "Mafia! Don't forget!"

SOMEONE WAS KNOCKING, and when my lamp wouldn't switch on I glided from my bed to the door in the dark without hitting a thing—my cramped, shabby rooms like just another part of my body, I'd lived in them so long. In the peephole swam a face I couldn't comprehend, a stretched-out Silly Putty face, unearthly pale, longer and more honest than a regular face. I was looking at a German shepherd, I realized. *Let me in,* a voice growled. The face didn't move.

"Happy-Go-Puppy," Eddie grunted when I cracked the door, and then he let the dog drop, heavily, onto its paws. The pony-sized animal nosed its way inside, pushing past my legs, while Eddie slapped water off his baseball cap. "Your whole complex is black," he said. "How long has it been out?"

"It must've gone out while I was asleep," I said. "This is a *stray*? I thought he was something for your act." The dog, solid white, looked rare and specially bred, something out of a circus, or a children's book, or a dream. Happy-Go-Puppy, the rescue group Eddie volunteered for, took in dogs the county shelter considered hard-adopts—because they were ugly, mean, retarded, terminally ill—in order to buy them some time, increase their chances of finding new owners. Sometimes I suspected Eddie thought of me as a hard-adopt. "Are you going to keep him?" I asked. "It would be complicated, making something that big disappear, wouldn't it?" The dog was casing the corners of the room like a crime-scene detective, luminous even in the pitch-black, as if he emitted his own light.

"No, I've only got him for the week," Eddie said. "He had his vestigial toe removed and they can't adopt him out till it heals. His name's Houdini, actually, but just because he escapes all the time. He doesn't do tricks—not even obedience-trained. What I want to know is what happened to the damn electricity. All it's doing is raining. It's like the power company doesn't even *try*."

I mixed whiskey sours, trying to get the proportions by feel, and skipped telling about getting fired. I reported instead on the repair guy—his invitation, his face, the way he'd shaken out his shoulders, the way everything seemed so perfect in that single moment. *If you could see him, you'd understand everything,* I kept saying, waiting for Eddie to jump in, encourage me like he always did to just *go, give the guy a chance,* but he was silent, standing beside me screwing the tops back on bottles. I imagined his expression, a smug combination of pity and disdain. *Okay, fine, I'm pathetic,* I thought, *but you don't have to be so judgmental, just because you never have to diet, because you've got a boyfriend.* I hadn't planned to mention that subject, but I felt a rush of impatience all of a sudden. "So, why don't you let me make you guys dinner sometime, you and this Mary K. guy," I said. "Or just meet you out somewhere—we could see his show. I mean, I don't know what you're so worried about, but I think I should get to meet him, if he's so special—"

"He's not," Eddie said. "I'm totally over him."

"What are you talking about? Wasn't that him, at your place, before? You could've brought him with you—"

"It's *over,* okay? God, I wish the power would come on."

Then, with a buzzing hum, it did. Just for a flash, *one Mississippi, two Mississippi,* enough time to see, in the yellow-flooded kitchen, Eddie's ruined face. The bright red-purple swell of new bruises, a patternless pattern, a broken splash across his pretty features, as if someone had grabbed his face and twisted, crumpled it like an empty bag. Then the hum crescendoed, banged, and cut off, and the room fell dark again. The dog's collar jangled in the hallway, moving tentatively toward us.

"Sounds like a transformer blew," Eddie said.

"What happened?" I said. "What *happened*?"

He didn't ask what I meant. "This dog," he said, "has really been through it. Would you believe he was born in Puerto Rico? Belonged to an old man who lived in a shack on the beach and rode his bike up and down the boardwalk all day, panhandling. When the guy died the dog lived on his own for weeks, just hanging out with all the homeless people. They all knew him. But then some damned tourists found him and took him home, convinced the beach people they'd take care of him, only once they got him here they just stuck him in the yard and quit feeding him. Didn't want hair on the furniture, they told the pound. That's how he learned to jump fences. And slip out of harnesses. And hold in his pee, so he wouldn't get dehydrated. It's a bitch to get him to pee, now. You can see it makes him really nervous."

"It was my fault, I started it," he added after a moment, when I didn't say anything. "I shoved him out of my water bed. He called me *repulsive*. Can you believe that? *Repulsive*. Whatever! Anyway, I'm fine, I'm over him already."

"What did he *do*?" I said. "Do you want to go to the emergency room—or call the police?" I felt the dog leaning against my knees and reached to pet him, trying not to picture what happened, picture it happening.

"He likes to lean," Eddie said. "That's a big dog thing, they just like to feel something bigger than themselves, I think."

"Where is he now?" I said. "Is he still at your place?"

"Are you kidding?" Eddie said. "It's over, just forget about it."

"Well, I can't believe it," I said.

"Well, honey, believe it," he said. He took his drink from me, our wet fingertips overlapping. The outline of his head bent toward the cup, then quickly up and back. "I mean, it wasn't the first time."

"What!"

"Please, will you spare me? Don't act so shocked. I mean, it's not like you haven't been there."

"I've been there," I said. "Which is why I don't go there anymore. I mean, I had no idea—I thought you were going to move in with this guy, or something."

"You live in a fantasy world," he said. "Give me a refill, will you? Look, when I was a kid, there was this rumor, one of those urban legends, that there was a Miss Nude America pageant that came on TV really late at night, after the regular Miss America pageant was over. We all thought if we could just stay awake long enough, sneak out of bed or trick our parents into letting us stay up, we'd see it—we talked about it for like a *year*. We weren't that young, no one believed in Santa Claus or anything like that anymore, but this was, like, the most exciting thing anyone ever heard of."

"I never heard of it," I said.

"That's not the point. The point is, nobody ever saw it, and nobody freaked out—eventually it just kind of faded away. Everyone just kind of figured it out. At some point, you just give up the ghost and grow up and face reality— it's called *surviving*."

"You didn't give up the ghost," I snapped. "You're a magician—that's the opposite of reality. You own a *rabbit*. Don't try to pretend you're cynical."

"That's different," he said. "Magic's a job, it doesn't kick your ass. I'm just saying, we can't be girls forever—we're over thirty-five, remember? It's not attractive after a certain point. If you want to quit getting disillusioned, give up your illusions."

You're wrong, I thought. The AC guy just existing, not even doing anything, just glancing at me, made me a girl again, as much a girl as I'd ever been. *Poof!* Just like one of your tricks. "I never claimed to be attractive," I said. I had sunk, cross-legged, onto the linoleum, and Houdini came over and settled himself upright in my lap, staring straight ahead and spilling over on every side, his white shoulder filling my field of vision. He seemed unaware of his own size.

"Hey, *I* think you're attractive," Eddie slurred. "I'm your best friend, remember? Hey, you want that dog? He's useless to me, so if you want him, please, feel free."

"He's that guy's dog, isn't he," I said.

"Yeah, I got his fucking dog," Eddie said. "But the rest of

it, everything else, the old man with the bicycle, the home-less people, holding in his pee, that's all true."

"I'll keep him," I said. My complex would never allow it, my lease was month-to-month, I had no yard, my rooms were too small, I had no job.

"I'll take him back tomorrow," Eddie said.

"You can't," I said. "You shouldn't go *near* this guy. If he's abusive—"

"He doesn't beat the dog," Eddie said.

"But what if he does?"

"He doesn't. It's his dog. You can't hide a dog like this."

"He doesn't *deserve* the dog."

I felt Eddie kiss my cheek, a small wet connection in the dark, and I realized I'd been arguing with my eyes closed. "Don't worry about it," he said into my ear. "I'm fine, the dog is fine. Pretend you never saw me. Pretend I didn't tell you anything. Tell me about your new boyfriend."

"Nothing to tell," I said. I locked my arms around the animal and pulled him, unflinching, against my heart. He leaned, a thoughtful, steady pressure. "I'll never see that guy again," I said, knowing as I said it it was true. It was just better this way.

• • •

I woke up on my sofa at dawn, Houdini still curled against me, dream-twitching. My digital clocks were flashing, and I saw ragged patches of clear sky outside, and Eddie's shiny black head on my pillow in the other room. When I started crying, the dog opened his eyes and sighed heavily through his nostrils, looking not at me but at the ceiling as if in resignation, like he'd heard this a million times. He stretched his legs between mine, exquisitely, as if my weeping were a lovely lulling thing, predictable as waves or rain.

I had just nodded off again when my downstairs neighbor, the Iranian student, banged his bike out onto the porch like he did every morning, rattling his keys and noisily throwing his deadbolt, then creaking the bike into motion. In one move, Houdini raised and disentangled himself, landed on all four paws, and streaked to the door, where he stood, frozen, head held high, eyes flooded with recognition, listening to the unmistakable *click-click-click* of that bicycle chain as it moved slowly off into the street, and away. I called his name, softly, but he didn't look.

I remembered that childhood rhyme: *Yesterday upon the stair, I met a man who wasn't there, he wasn't there again today, I wish that man would go away.* But there was

nothing I could say to help the dog, no way for me to explain, or even let him know I understood, and I wondered
if this was how God felt, knowing all our stories as He supposedly did, yet unwilling or unable, for reasons He refused
to reveal, to make them make sense.